AF521180

Truth [Vérité]

Book II

by

Émile Zola

Double9 BOOKS

Truth [Vérité]

Book II

by Émile Zola

Copyright © 2024

All Rights reserved.

No part of this publication may be reproduced, stored in a retrieval system, or transmitted in any form or by any means, electronic, mechanical, photocopying or Otherwise, without the written permission of the publisher.
The author/editor asserts the moral right to be identified as the author/editor of this work.

ISBN: 978-93-68090-24-3

Published by

DOUBLE 9 BOOKS
2/13-B, Ansari Road
Daryaganj, New Delhi – 110002
info@double9books.com
www.double9books.com
Tel. 011-40042856

This book is under public domain

ABOUT THE AUTHOR

Émile Zola was a French novelist, journalist, and the most prominent figure in the literary school of naturalism. Zola is best known for his detailed and unflinching depictions of French society. His works explore themes of social injustice, human nature, and the influence of environment and heredity on personal fate.Zola's most famous work is the Les Rougon-Macquart series, a sprawling cycle of 20 novels that trace the lives of multiple generations of a family, set against the backdrop of Second Empire France. The series includes notable works like Germinal, a powerful novel about coal miners' struggles, Thérèse Raquin, a dark tale of passion and murder, and The Downfall (La Débâcle), which explores the impact of the Franco-Prussian War. His work was a critical reflection on the failings of society, and he championed the rights of the working class and the oppressed Zola's influence on literature was immense, and his works are considered foundational to the naturalist movement.

CONTENTS

CHAPTER I

One sunny morning in May Marc, for the first time, took his class at Maillebois. On the side facing the square, the large schoolroom had three lofty windows, through whose panes of ground glass streamed a gay, white, and vivid light. In front of the master's desk, which stood on a small platform reached by three steps, the boys' little double desks were set out, four in each of the eight rows.

Loud laughter, in fact quite an uproar, burst forth when one of the lads, on proceeding to his seat, stumbled and fell intentionally.

'Now, boys,' Marc quietly said, 'you must behave yourselves. I am not going to punish you, but you will find it more beneficial and pleasant to behave yourselves with me.... Monsieur Mignot, please call the register.'

Marc had wished to have Mignot's assistance on this first occasion, and the other's demeanour plainly indicated his hostility and the surprise he felt at having as his principal a man who had compromised himself so greatly in the recent scandals. Mignot had even joined in the boys' laughter when one of them had stumbled and fallen by way of amusing the others. However, the calling of the register began.

'Auguste Doloir!'

'Present!' exclaimed a merry-looking lad in so gruff a voice that the whole class again exploded.

Auguste was the mason's elder son, and it was he who had stumbled a few minutes previously. Nine years of age, he looked vigorous and intelligent, but he was wrong-headed, and his pranks often revolutionised the school.

'Charles Doloir!' called Mignot.

'Present!' And this time Auguste's brother, two years his junior, answered in so shrill a voice that the storm of laughter began afresh. Though Charles was of a more refined and gentle nature than Auguste, he invariably seconded him.

But Marc let the matter pass. He wished to be patient and to inflict no punishments that first day. While the calling of the register proceeded he glanced round the large room where he would have to deal with all those turbulent lads. At Jonville there had been no such lavish provision of blackboards—one behind his desk for himself, and two others, right and left, for the boys—nor such a display of coloured prints representing weights and measures, the mineral, vegetable, and animal kingdoms, useful and harmful insects, mushrooms and toadstools, without counting the large and numerous maps. There, too, in a cabinet was a collection of the 'solid bodies,' as well as various instruments for the teaching of physics and chemistry. But Marc did not find among his new pupils the good understanding and cordiality which had prevailed among those whom he had left at Jonville. The neglect of his weak and ailing predecessor, Méchain, had evidently helped to disorganise the school, which, after numbering nearly sixty pupils, could now muster scarcely forty. Thus its position was sorely compromised, and the hard task of restoring it to prosperity and orderliness lay before him.

'Achille Savin!' Mignot called.

There was no answer, and he therefore repeated the name. Yet both the Savins, the twin sons of the tax-collector's clerk, sat at one of the double desks, with their heads lowered and a sly expression on their faces. Though they were only eight years of age they seemed already proficient in prudent hypocrisy.

'Achille and Philippe Savin!' Mignot repeated, glancing at them.

Thereupon, making up their minds, they answered leisurely but in unison, 'Present!'

Marc, who felt surprised, inquired why they had previously remained silent; but he could obtain no answer from them; they looked at him distrustfully as if they had to defend themselves from him.

'Fernand Bongard!' Mignot continued.

Again nobody answered. Fernand, the peasant farmer's son, a sturdy boy of ten, sat there huddled up, leaning on his elbows, with a stupefied expression on his face. He seemed to be sleeping with his eyes open. But one of his schoolfellows gave him a nudge, and then in a scared way he shouted 'Present!'

This time none of the others dared to laugh, for they feared Fernand's fists. And, silence continuing, Mignot was able to call the last name: 'Sébastien Milhomme!'

Marc had already recognised Madame Alexandre's son. Eight years of age, with a face all gentleness, refinement, and intelligence, he sat at the first desk on the right hand. And the young man smiled at the lad; charmed by his candid eyes, in which he fancied he could detect the early sparkle of a young mind, such as he desired to awaken.

'Present!' Sébastien answered in a clear gay voice, which to Marc seemed like music compared with all the full or mocking voices of the others.

The calling of the register was finished; and at a sign from Mignot all the boys now rose for prayers. Since Simon's departure, Méchain had allowed prayers to be said at the beginning and the end of each class, yielding, in this respect, to the stealthy persuasion of Mademoiselle Rouzaire, who, citing her own practice as an example, asserted that the fear of hell greatly helped to keep her pupils quiet. Moreover, parents were pleased with the prayer-saying, and Mauraisin, the Elementary Inspector, regarded it with favour, although it in no wise figured in the regulations. That morning, however, Marc swiftly intervened, saying in his quiet and resolute way: 'Sit down, boys. You are not here to say prayers. You may say them at home if your fathers and mothers desire it.'

Mignot, nonplussed, looked at him inquisitively. Ah! well, he would not exercise much authority at Maillebois if he began by suppressing prayers! Marc fully understood the meaning of his assistant's glance, for ever since his arrival in the little town he had been conscious of the general feeling, the conviction that he was destined to encounter rapid and complete defeat. Besides, Salvan had warned him, and had recommended extreme prudence, a course of skilful tolerance during the first months. If Marc, after due reflection, ventured to suppress prayers, it was as a first step, the result of which would enable him to feel his way. He would have liked to remove the big crucifix which Méchain, exhausted by the pressure brought to bear on him, had allowed to be hung over the blackboard behind the master's desk. But the young man felt that he could hardly do that immediately; it was necessary that he should establish himself firmly in his position and know his ground thoroughly before he engaged in a real battle. Apart from the crucifix he was also irritated by four glaring chromolithographs which hung from the walls, one of them representing the fable of St. Geneviève delivering Paris, another Joan of Arc listening to the voices from heaven, another St. Louis healing the sick by the touch of his hands, and another Napoleon riding across a battlefield. Miracle and force, religious lie and military violence were ever given as examples, ever sown as seed in the minds of the children who would become the citizens of to-morrow. Marc asked himself if all that ought not to be changed, if education ought not to be begun afresh at the very beginning, with lessons of truth and solidarity, if one was to create free and intelligent men, capable of practising justice.

The first class was duly held, Marc gently yet firmly taking possession of his post among his new pupils, whose curiosity he found tinged with rebellion. The pacific conquest of their minds and hearts which the young master desired to effect proceeded patiently day by day. At the outset he occasionally experienced some secret bitterness, for his mind wandered back to the well-loved pupils, the children of his brain, whom he had left at Jonville, and whom he knew to be now in the hands of one of his former colleagues, Jauffre, with whose spirit of intrigue and thirst for immediate success he was well acquainted. He felt some remorse at the thought that he had abandoned his work yonder to one who would surely destroy it, and his only consolation lay in the circumstance that he had taken up yet more pressing and necessary work at Maillebois. To that work he became more and more passionately attached, devoting himself to it with enthusiastic faith as the days flew by and lesson followed lesson.

On the morrow of the General Elections, which took place during that month of May, quietude fell upon the region. Prior to those elections silence and restraint with respect to Simon's case had been declared imperative, in order that the result of the polling might not prove disastrous for the Republic; and directly those elections were over—the new Chamber of Deputies being composed of virtually the same men as the previous one—silence was again declared to be necessary, lest, by raising inopportune questions, one should retard the realisation of promised reforms. The truth was that after all the battling of the electoral campaign the successful candidates desired to enjoy the dearly-bought fruits of victory in peace. Thus, at Beaumont, neither Lemarrois nor Marcilly, on being re-elected, was willing to mention Simon's name, although each had promised to act as soon as his mandate should be renewed and he should no longer have to fear the blindness of universal suffrage. But at present it was held that Simon had been judged and well judged; in fact the slightest allusion to his affair was deemed contrary to patriotism. Naturally enough the same views prevailed at Maillebois. Darras, the Mayor, even begged Marc, in the interest of the unhappy prisoner and his relatives, to do nothing whatever, but to wait for some wakening of public opinion. Meantime absolute forgetfulness was effected, perfect silence was enjoined, as if there were no Simonists or anti-Simonists left.

Marc had to resign himself to the position, particularly as he was entreated in that sense by the ever humble and anxious Lehmanns, and even by David, who, with all his heroic tenacity, understood the necessity of patience. Yet Simon's brother was now following up a serious clue.

Indirectly and without positive proof thereof, he had heard of the illegal communication which President Gragnon had made to the jury in their retiring room prior to the verdict; and if he could only establish the fact that this communication had been really made, the annulment of all the proceedings would necessarily follow. But David was conscious of the difficulties of the times, and prosecuted his inquiries with the greatest secrecy for fear of warning his adversaries. Marc, though of a more feverish spirit, at last consented to follow the same tactics and feign forgetfulness. Thus the Simon affair began to slumber as if it were ended and forgotten, whereas, in reality, it remained the secret sore, the poisoned, incurable wound of which the social body—ever exposed to the danger of some sudden and mortal outburst of delirium—was dying. For, be it remembered, one single act of injustice may suffice for a whole nation to be stricken with dementia and slowly die.

In this position of affairs Marc for a time was able to devote himself entirely to his school duties, and he did so with the conviction that he was contributing to the only work by which iniquity may be destroyed and its renewal prevented—that work which consists in diffusing knowledge and sowing the seeds of truth among the rising generations. Never before had he understood so fully the terrible difficulties of the task. He found himself utterly alone. He felt that his pupils and their parents, his assistant Mignot, and his neighbour Mademoiselle Rouzaire were all against him. And the times were disastrous; the Brothers' school recruited five more pupils from the Communal school during Marc's first month. A blast of unpopularity threatened to sweep the young man away. Parents went to the Ignorantines in order to save their children from the abominations of that new secular master who had suppressed prayers on the very day he had entered upon his functions. Thus Brother Fulgence was quite triumphant. He was again assisted by Brothers Gorgias and Isidore, who had disappeared for a while after Simon's trial, and who now had been recalled, by way of showing, no doubt, that the community deemed itself to be above suspicion. If Brother Lazarus, the third assistant, had not returned to Maillebois with the others, the reason was that he had died during his absence. The others remained the masters of the town, whose streets were always full of cassocks.

For Marc the worst was the mocking contempt with which all those folk seemed to regard him. They did not condescend to make any violent attack on him, they waited for him to commit suicide by some act of stupendous folly. Mignot's demeanour on the first day had become that of the whole district. As Mademoiselle Rouzaire said, it was expected that Marc would render his position untenable in less than two months. The young man detected the hopes of his adversaries by the manner in which Inspector Mauraisin spoke to him on the occasion of his first visit. Mauraisin, knowing that Marc was covered by Salvan and Le Barazer, displayed a kind of ironical indulgence, allowing the young man to follow his own course, but watching stealthily for some serious blunder which would enable him to apply for his removal to another part. He said nothing about the suppression of prayers, he desired something more decisive, an *ensemble* of crushing facts. The Inspector was seen laughing over the matter with Mademoiselle Rouzaire, one of his favourites, and from that moment Marc was surrounded by spies, eager to denounce both his expressions of opinion and his actions.

Every time that Marc called upon Salvan in search of a little comfort, his protector repeated to him: 'Be prudent, my friend.... Yesterday Le Barazer received another anonymous letter denouncing you as a poisoner and a henchman of hell. You know that I wish all success to the good work, but I also think that it may be compromised by precipitate action. As a beginning, render yourself necessary, bring back affluence to the school, get yourself liked.'

At this Marc, however bitter his feelings, ended by smiling: 'You are right, I feel it is so,' he answered; 'it is by force of wisdom and affection that one must conquer.'

He, Geneviève, and little Louise were now dwelling in the quarters formerly allotted to Simon. The lodging was larger and more comfortable than that of Jonville. There were two bedrooms and two sitting-rooms, besides a kitchen and dependencies. And the whole was very clean and very bright, full of sunshine, and overlooked a fairly large garden in which vegetables and flowers grew. But the young couple's furniture was scanty; and since their quarrel with Madame Duparque, it was difficult for them to make both ends meet, for Marc's meagre salary was all they had to depend upon. That salary now amounted to twelve hundred francs a year, but it really represented no more than the thousand francs allowed at Jonville, for there Marc had also received payment as parish clerk, which post was not to be thought of at Maillebois. And how were they to manage on a hundred francs a month in that little town where living was more expensive than in the village? How were they to maintain some little appearance of dignity and comfort? How was Marc to wear fairly respectable frock coats, such as usage demanded? It was a grave problem, the solution of which required prodigies of thrift, continuous secret heroism in all the petty details of life. They often ate dry bread in order that they might have clean linen.

But, in Geneviève, Marc found a valuable, an admirable helpmate. She renewed the exploits she had accomplished at Jonville, she managed to provide for all the requirements of the home, without allowing much of its penury to be seen. She had to attend to everything—cooking, washing, and mending—and Louise was ever all smiles and smartness in her light-hued little frocks. If Mignot, according to usage, had taken his meals with his principal, the money paid for his board might have helped Geneviève slightly. But the young bachelor, who had his own quarters on the other side of the landing, preferred to patronise a neighbouring eating-house, perhaps in order to mark his hostility and to avoid compromising himself by any companionship with a man for whom Mademoiselle Rouzaire predicted the worst catastrophes. He, Mignot, with his paltry monthly salary of seventy-one francs and twenty-five centimes, [1] led the usual wretched life of a young assistant-master, ill clad and ill fed, with no other diversion within his reach than that of fishing on Thursdays and Sundays. This rendered him all the more ill-tempered and distrustful, as though indeed it were Marc's fault if he partook of such sorry messes at the eating-house. Yet Geneviève displayed solicitude for his welfare. She offered to mend his linen, and one evening, when he was suffering from a cold, she hastened to make him some herb-drink. As she and her husband said, the young fellow was not bad-hearted, he was badly advised. Perhaps, by showing him some kindness and equity, they might at last win him over to better sentiments.

[1] A little less than $14.

That which Geneviève dared not say, for fear of grieving Marc, was that the home suffered particularly from the quarrel with Madame Duparque. In former days the grandmother had provided Louise with clothes, made presents, and rendered assistance at difficult times. Now that the young people were at Maillebois, only a few doors distant from the old lady, she might often have helped them. Under the circumstances it was very embarrassing to live so near, and to be obliged to turn one's head aside every time one met her. On two occasions little Louise, who, being only three years of age, could not understand the situation, held out her arms and called when the old lady passed, in such wise that the fated reconciliation ended by taking place. Geneviève, on returning home one day, in a state of great emotion, related that she had yielded to circumstances and had embraced her grandmother and mother on meeting them on the Place des Capucins, where Louise, in all innocence, had run forward and cast herself into their arms.

At this confession Marc, in his turn, kissed his wife, saying with a good-natured smile: 'But that is all right, my darling. For your sake and Louise's I am well pleased with the reconciliation. It was bound to come, and if I am on bad terms with those ladies you surely don't imagine that I am such a barbarian as to demand the same of you.'

'No, my friend,' Geneviève replied, 'only it is very embarrassing in a family when the wife visits a place where her husband cannot go.'

'Why should it be embarrassing? For the sake of peace it is best that I should not call on your grandmother again, for I cannot possibly agree with her. But there is nothing to prevent you and the little one from visiting her and your mother also, from time to time.'

Geneviève had become grave, her eyes fell, and while she reflected she quivered.

'I should have preferred not to go to grandmother's without you,' she said. 'I feel firmer when we are together.... But you are right, I understand that it would be painful for you to accompany me, and, on the other hand, it is difficult for me to break off now.'

Thus the question was settled. At first Geneviève went but once a week to the little house on the Place des Capucins, taking Louise with her, and spending an hour there during the school work of Marc, who contented himself with bowing to the ladies when he met them.

And now, for a period of two years, with infinite patience and good nature, Marc prosecuted the conquest of his pupils amid hostile surroundings and innumerable worries. He was a born teacher, one who knew how to become a child again in order that children might understand him. And, in particular, he strove to be gay; he willingly joined in his pupils' play, behaving as if he were simply a companion, an elder brother. And in the school work his strength lay in his power to cast his science aside, to place himself within the reach of young and imperfectly awakened minds, by finding easy explanatory words suited to each occasion. It was as if he himself were still somewhat ignorant, and participated in the delight of learning. Heavily laden as the curriculum might be, what with reading, writing, grammar, orthography, composition, arithmetic, history, geography, elementary science, singing, gymnastics, notions of agriculture, manual work, morals and civic instruction, he passed nothing by until the lads had understood it. All his first efforts indeed were concentrated on method, in order that nothing taught might be lost, but that everything might be positively and fully assimilated.

Ah! how fervently did Marc devote himself to that sowing and cultivation of truth! He strove to plan things in such wise that truth might impose itself on his pupils by its own power, nourish their expanding minds, and become both their flesh and their brains. And what truth it was! It so happens that every error claims to be truth. Does not even the Roman Catholic Church, though based on absurd dogmas, pretend that it is the sole truth? Thus Marc began by teaching that there is no truth outside the pale of reason, logic, and particularly experiment. When the son of a peasant or a workman is told by his schoolmaster that the world is round and revolves in space, he accepts the statement upon trust just as he accepts the statements made to him by the priest on matters of religion at the Catechism class. In order that he may appreciate the difference, experiment must show him the scientific certainty of the former statement. All so-called revealed truth is falsehood; experimental truth alone is accurate—one, entire, eternal. Marc therefore at the outset found it necessary to rebut the Catholic catechism by the scientific catechism. He took the world and mankind as they were explained by science, and set them forth in their living reality and their march towards a continual and ever more and more perfect future. There was no possibility of real amelioration, liberation, and happiness otherwise than by truth—that is, by knowledge of the conditions in which mankind exists and progresses. All the craving for knowledge as a means for rapid attainment to health and peace bore within itself its method of free expansion, science ceasing to be a dead letter, and becoming a source of life, an excitant of temperament and character.

Marc, as far as possible, left books upon one side, in order to compel his pupils to judge things for themselves. They only knew things well when they had seen or touched them. He never asked them to believe in a phenomenon until he had proved its reality by experiment. The whole domain of unproven facts was set aside, in reserve, for future investigation. But he demonstrated that with the help of the acquired truths mankind might already rear for itself a large and splendid home of security and brotherliness. To see things for oneself, to convince oneself of what one ought to believe, to develop one's reasoning powers and one's individuality in accordance with the reasons of existence and action, such were the principles which governed Marc's teaching method, the only one by which true men might be created.

But knowledge was not sufficient—a social bond, a spiritual link of perpetual solidarity was required. And this Marc found in Justice. He had often noticed with what a flash of rebellion a boy, molested in his rights, would exclaim: 'That isn't fair!' Indeed, any act of injustice raises a tempest in the depths of those young minds, and brings them frightful suffering. This is because the idea of justice in them is absolute. Mark turned to good use the candour of equity, the innate need of truth and justice, that one finds in children when life has not yet inclined them to mendacious and iniquitous compromises. By way of Truth towards Justice—such was the road along which he strove to direct his pupils, as often as possible requiring them to judge themselves when they happened to be in fault. If they had told a falsehood, he made them admit the wrong they had done both to their schoolfellows and to themselves. If they were disorderly and delayed lessons, he showed them that they were the first to suffer. At times a culprit spontaneously admitted his offence, thus earning forgiveness. Emulation in equity ended by animating those young people; they learnt to rival one another in frankness. At times, of course, there was trouble, conflict, catastrophe, for all this was only a beginning, and several generations of schoolboys would be needed for schools to become the real abodes of healthy and happy life. Marc, however, rejoiced over the slightest results that he obtained, convinced as he was that if knowledge were primarily essential for all progress, nothing definitive with respect to the happiness of mankind could be achieved without the assistance of the spirit of justice. Why did the *bourgeois* class, which was the best educated, become rotten so soon? Was it not by reason of its iniquities, its denial of justice, its refusal to restore what it had stolen, to give to the humble and the suffering their legitimate share of the world's good things? Some folk, in condemning education, cited the ignominious downfall of the *bourgeoisie* as an example, and accused science of producing a multitude of casteless individuals, thereby increasing the sum of evil and tribulation. And yes, so long as the passion for knowledge merely for its own sake should become keener and keener in a social system which was all falsehood and injustice, it would only add to existing ruins. It was necessary that science should tend towards justice, and bring to the future city of fraternity a moral system of liberty and peace.

Even to be just did not suffice; Marc also required kindliness and affection of his pupils. Nothing could germinate, nothing could flower, unless it were by love and for it. In the universal flame of desire and union one found the focus of the world. Within each human being was implanted an imperious need to mingle with all others; and personal action, liberty, and individuality were like the play of different organs, all dependent on the universal Being. If each individual man, even when isolated, represented so much will and power, his actions, at all events, only began to count when they exercised an influence on the community. To love, to make oneself loved, to make all others love: the teacher's *rôle* was found entire in those three propositions, those three degrees of human instruction. To love—Marc loved his pupils with his whole heart, giving himself to them unreservedly, knowing full well that one must indeed love if one would teach, for only love has the power of touching and convincing. To make oneself loved—that was a task to which he devoted every hour, fraternising with his boys, never seeking to make them fear him, but, on the contrary, striving to win them over by persuasion, affection, the good-fellowship of an elder brother still growing up among his juniors. To make all others love—that again was his constant thought; he was ever recalling the true saying that the happiness of each is compounded of the happiness of all; and he brought forward the daily example of the progress and pleasure of each boy when the whole class had worked well.

Schooling, no doubt, should have as its objects the culture of energy, the liberation and exaltation of each individuality; a child must judge and act by himself alone in order that as a man he may yield the sum-total of his personal value. But, as Marc put it, would not the crop resulting from such intensive culture increase the common harvest of all? Could a man create true glory for himself without contributing in one or another form to the happiness of others? Education necessarily tended to solidarity, to the universal attraction which was gradually blending mankind into one family. And Marc's mind and heart were set on sympathy and affection, on a joyous, brotherly school, full of sunshine, song, and laughter, where happiness was taught, where the pupils learnt to live the life of science, truth, and justice, which would come in all its fulness when the way for it should have been sufficiently prepared by generations of children taught as they ought to be.

From the very outset Marc combated the system by which violence, terror, and folly were inculcated in so many children. The right of the stronger, massacre, carnage, the devastation and razing of cities—all those things were set before the young, glorified in books, pictures, and constant, almost hourly, lessons. Great was the display of the bloody pages of history, the wars, the conquests, the names of the captains who had butchered their fellow-beings. The minds of children were enfevered by the crash of arms, by nightmares of slaughter steeping the plains in blood. In the prize books given to them, in the little papers published for their perusal, on the very covers of their copybooks, their eyes encountered the savagery of armies, the burning of fleets, the everlasting calamity of man sinking to the level of a wolf. And when a battle was not depicted there came a miracle, some absurd legend, some source of darkness: a saint delivering a country by his or her prayers, an intervention of Jesus or Mary ensuring the ownership of the world to the wealthy, a Churchman solving political and social difficulties by a mere sign of the Cross. The humble were invariably warned that they must show obedience and resignation. To impress it on their minds in childhood's hour, stormy skies were shown them, illumined by the lightning of an irritated and cruel Deity. Terror reigned, terror of that Deity, terror too of the devil, a base and hideous terror, which seized on man in his infancy and kept him cowering until he reached the grave after a life which was all dense night, ignorance, and falsehood. In that manner one fashioned only slaves, flesh fit to serve the master's capricious purposes. And indeed that education of blind faith and perpetual extermination was based on the necessity of ever having soldiers ready to defend the established and iniquitous order of things.

Yet what an antiquated idea it was to cultivate human energy by lessons of warfare! It corresponded with the times when the sword alone decided questions between nation and nation, and between kings and their subjects. But nowadays, if nations still guard themselves—as they do, in formidable fashion, full of anxious dread lest everything should collapse—who will dare to say that victory will rest with the warlike nations? Who, on the contrary, cannot see that the triumphant nation of to-morrow will be that which defeats the others on the economic field, by reorganising the conditions of human toil, and by bringing more justice and happiness to mankind?

To Marc it seemed that the only worthy *rôle* for France was that of completing the Revolution and becoming the great emancipator. The narrow doctrine that one's sole purpose should be to make soldiers of Frenchmen filled him with grief and anger. On the morrow of the disasters of 1870 such a programme may have had its excuse; and yet all the unrest of years and years, the whole abominable crisis of the present times has proceeded from that programme, from having placed one's supreme hope in the army, from having abandoned the democracy to military leaders. If it be still necessary to guard oneself, surrounded as one is by neighbours in arms, it is yet more necessary to become workers, free and just citizens, such as those to whom to-morrow will belong. On the day when France knows it and wills it, on the day when she becomes a nation freed from error, the armour-plated empires around her will crumble beneath the breath of truth and justice emanating from her lips—a breath which will achieve that which can never be accomplished by all her armies and her guns. Nations awaken nations, and on the day when, one by one, the nations rise, enlightened, instructed by example, the world will witness the victory of peace, the end of war. Marc could imagine for his country no more splendid *rôle* than that of hastening the day when all countries would mingle in one. Thus he kept a strict watch over his pupils' books, replacing as far as possible all pictures and descriptions of spurious miracles and bloody battles by others which dealt with the truths of science and the fruitful labours of mankind. The one true source of energy lies in work for happiness' sake.

In the course of the second year some good results were already manifest. Dividing his school into two classes, Marc took charge of the first, composed of boys from nine to thirteen years of age, while Mignot attended to the second, in which the lads were from six to nine years old. The young principal also adopted the system of appointing monitors, whence he derived certain advantages, a saving of time in some matters, and an increase of emulation among his boys. Not a moment was lost during school hours, yet he allowed the lads as much independence as possible, chatting with them, provoking objections from them, and imposing nothing on them by dint of authority, desirous as he was that all feeling of certainty should come from their own minds. Thus gaiety prevailed, and the lessons in which those young minds passed from discovery to discovery were full of attractiveness.

On one matter only did Marc insist, and that was great cleanliness. Under his guidance the lads took pleasure in washing their hands at the water taps, and the classroom windows were opened widely at each interval between lessons, as well as afterwards. Before Marc's time it had been the practice (a usual one in French elementary schools) for the boys to sweep the schoolroom floor, whereby they raised a terrible amount of dust,—a redoubtable means of spreading contagion,—but he taught them to wash the floor with sponges, a duty which they soon regarded as a pastime.

One sunshiny day in May, two years after Marc's appointment to Maillebois, Inspector Mauraisin paid the school a surprise visit during the interval between morning lessons. It was in vain that he had hitherto kept a watch on Marc. He was disconcerted by the young man's prudence, infuriated by his inability to send in a bad report such as would have justified removal. That clumsy revolutionary dreamer, whom nobody had expected to see six months in office, was becoming a perfect fixture, to the amazement and scandal of all right-thinking people. By devising that surprise visit, however, the Inspector hoped to catch him in fault.

As it happened, the boys had just been washing the classroom floor, and handsome little Mauraisin, sprucely buttoned up in his frock coat, raised a cry of alarm: 'What! are you flooded?'

When Marc explained that he had replaced sweeping by washing, for reasons of hygiene, the Inspector shrugged his shoulders: 'Another novelty!' said he. 'You might at least have warned the Administration. Besides, all this water cannot be healthy, it must tend to rheumatism. You will please content yourself with the broom so long as you are not authorised to use sponges.'

Then, as the interval between lessons was not quite over, he began to rummage everywhere, even opening the cupboards to see if their contents were in order. Perhaps he hoped to find some bad books, some Anarchist pamphlets. At all events he criticised everything, laid stress on the slightest sign of negligence, passing censure in a loud voice, in the very midst of the boys, by way of humiliating Marc in their presence. At last, the boys having resumed their seats, the usual questioning began.

Mauraisin's first attack fell upon Mignot because little Charles Doloir, eight years of age, and therefore in the second class, was unable to answer a question on a subject which he had not yet studied.

'So you are behindhand with the programme!' said the Inspector. 'Why, your pupils ought to have reached that lesson two months ago.'

Mignot, who, though he stood there in a respectful attitude, was plainly irritated by the other's aggressive tone, turned towards his principal. It was indeed at the latter that Mauraisin had really aimed his remark. And so the young head-master replied: 'Excuse me, Monsieur l'Inspecteur, it was I who thought it right to intervert certain parts of the programme in order to make some of the lessons clearer. Besides, is it not better to attend less to the exact order of the lessons as given in the books than to their spirit, in such wise, however, that all may be taught to the boys in the course of the year?'

Mauraisin affected great indignation: 'What! you interfere with the programme, monsieur? You, yourself, decide what to take of it and what to leave out? You substitute your fancy for the wisdom of your superiors? Well, they shall know that this class is behindhand.'

Then, his glance falling on the elder Doloir, Auguste, who was ten years old, he told him to stand up, and began to question him about the Reign of Terror, asking him to name the leaders of the period, Robespierre, Danton, Marat.

'Was Marat handsome, my boy?' he inquired.

Now Auguste Doloir, though Marc had succeeded in obtaining a little better behaviour from him, was still the rebel and trickster of the school. Either from ignorance or roguishness, it was hard to say, he now made answer: 'Oh! very handsome, monsieur.'

His schoolfellows, vastly amused, laughed and wriggled on their seats.

'No, no, my boy!' exclaimed Mauraisin, 'Marat was hideous, with every vice and every crime stamped upon his countenance!' And, turning towards Marc, he added clumsily enough: 'You do not teach them that Marat was handsome, I imagine!'

'No, Monsieur l'Inspecteur,' the master answered with a smile.

Laughter arose once more, and Mignot had to step between the desks to restore order, while Mauraisin, clinging to the subject of Marat, began to refer to Charlotte Corday. As luck would have it, he addressed himself to

Fernand Bongard, now a tall boy of eleven, whom he probably imagined to be one of the most advanced pupils.

'Here! you big fellow yonder, can you tell me how Marat died?'

He could not have been more unlucky. It was only with the greatest difficulty that Marc taught Fernand anything. The lad was not merely thick-headed, he did not try to learn, and as for the names and dates of history he was on the worst possible terms with them. He rose with a scared expression in his dilated eyes.

'Come, compose yourself, my boy,' said Mauraisin. 'Did not Marat die under peculiar circumstances?'

Fernand remained silent, with his mouth wide open. But a compassionate schoolfellow behind him whispered: 'In a bath'; whereupon in a very loud voice he answered: 'Marat drowned himself while taking a bath.'

This time the laughter became delirium, and Mauraisin flew into a temper: 'These boys are really stupid!' he exclaimed. 'Marat was killed in his bath by Charlotte Corday, a young girl of high-strung nature, who sacrificed herself in order to save France from a monster thirsting for blood.... Are you taught nothing, then, as you cannot answer the simplest questions?'

However, he interrogated the twin brothers Savin, Achille and Philippe, respecting the religious wars, and obtained fairly satisfactory answers from them. They were scarcely popular in the school, for not only were they sly and addicted to falsehoods, but they denounced those of their schoolfellows whom they saw in fault, besides telling their father of everything that occurred. Nevertheless the Inspector, won over by their hypocritical ways, cited them as examples: 'These boys know at least something,' said he. And again addressing himself to Philippe he inquired: 'Now, can you tell me what one ought to do to follow one's religion properly?'

'One ought to go to Mass, monsieur.'

'No doubt, but that is not sufficient; one ought to do everything that religion teaches. You hear, my boy—everything that religion teaches.'

Marc looked at Mauraisin in stupefaction, still he did not intervene, for he guessed that the Inspector in putting that singular question had been prompted by a desire to make him compromise himself by some imprudent remark. Indeed, that was so fully the other's object that he continued aggressively, addressing himself this time to Sébastien Milhomme: 'You, the little boy yonder with the fair hair, tell me what religion teaches?'

Sébastien, who stood erect, with an expression of consternation on his face, made no answer. He was the best pupil of the class, with a quick, intelligent mind, and an affectionate and gentle disposition. His inability to answer the Inspector brought tears to his eyes. As he received no lessons in religion, he did not even understand what he was asked.

'Well, you need not look at me like that, you little stupid!' exclaimed Mauraisin; 'my question is clear enough.'

But Marc was unable to restrain himself any longer. The embarrassment of his best pupil, to whom he was growing extremely attached, proved unbearable to him. So he came to his help: 'Excuse me, Monsieur l'Inspecteur, the teachings of religion are contained in the Church Catechism, and the Catechism is not included in our programme. So how can the lad answer you?'

This answer, no doubt, was what Mauraisin had expected. 'I have no lessons to receive from you, Monsieur le Maître,' he responded, feigning anger once more, 'I know what I am about. There is no properly conducted school in which a child cannot give a general answer to a question about the religion of his country.'

'I repeat. Monsieur l'Inspecteur,' rejoined Marc in a firm voice, in which a little rising anger became apparent, 'I repeat that it is not for me to teach the Catechism. You are mistaken, you are not at the school of the Brothers of the Christian Doctrine, who make the Catechism the basis of all their teaching. You are in a secular Republican school, expressly set apart from all the churches—one where the teaching is based solely on reason and science. If it be necessary, I shall appeal on the subject to my superiors.'

Mauraisin understood that he had gone too far. Each time that he had endeavoured to shake Marc's position he had found his superior, Academy Inspector Le Barazer, tacitly, passively supporting the young man, refusing to take any action against him unless grave and well-proven charges were brought forward. Moreover, Mauraisin knew Le Barazer's opinions respecting the absolute neutrality of the schools in religious matters. And so, without insisting on the subject, he curtailed his inspection, soon bringing it to an end, though not without again indulging in criticisms, for he was determined to find nothing satisfactory. The boys themselves deemed him ridiculous, and covertly made merry over the bad temper of that vain little fop whose hair and beard were so sprucely kept. When he withdrew, Mignot went so far as to shrug his shoulders, and whisper to Marc: 'We shall have a bad report, but you were quite right. That man is becoming altogether too stupid.'

For some time now, Mignot, gained upon by Marc's firm yet gentle behaviour, had been coming over to his side. It was not that he as yet shared his opinions in all things, for he was still anxious respecting his own advancement; but he had a sound mind at bottom, and was gradually yielding to the other's good guidance.

'Oh! a bad report!' Marc repeated gaily; 'he won't dare to venture beyond hypocritical and venomous attacks.... Ah! do you see him going into Mademoiselle Rouzaire's? He's with his divinity now. The worst is that his behaviour is not dictated by principle, but merely by personal policy, a desire to make his way in the world.'

At each inspection Mauraisin lavished very favourable reports upon Mademoiselle Rouzaire. She, at all events, took her girls to church, compelled them to recite the Catechism in school hours, and allowed the Inspector to question them about religion as much as he desired. One of her pupils, little Hortense Savin, who was being prepared for her first Communion, quite astonished Mauraisin by her extensive knowledge of Bible history. And if Angèle Bongard, thick-skulled like her brother, showed less proficiency in spite of her painfully stubborn efforts to learn, on the other hand Lucile Doloir, a little lass six years of age, who had joined the school only recently, gave promise of great intelligence, and would make, later on, a very charming 'Handmaiden of the Virgin.'

When morning lessons were over, Marc again caught sight of Mauraisin, whom Mademoiselle Rouzaire was escorting to the threshold of her school. They lingered there together, chatting in an intimate way and making gestures suggestive of great distress of mind. They were undoubtedly deploring what went on in the neighbouring boys' school, which was still in the hands of the disgraceful master of whom, for two years, they had been vainly trying to rid the town.

After long expecting the sudden removal of Marc, Maillebois was now growing accustomed to his presence. At a sitting of the Municipal Council, Mayor Darras had even found an opportunity to praise him; and his position had been strengthened recently by an incident of considerable significance: the return of two boys who had been previously transferred to the Brothers' school. This indicated that parents felt tranquillised, and were disposed to accept the young man, and it was also a check for the Congregational school, hitherto so prosperous and victorious. Was Marc about to succeed, then, in restoring the secular school to honour, by dint of wisdom and affection, as he had said to Salvan? Anxiety must have arisen among the Ignorantines and the monks, the whole clerical faction, for the young man suddenly found himself attacked in so singular a fashion that he was quite surprised. Mauraisin, on calling upon the Mayor and others, had left the Catechism question on one side, speaking only of Marc's new system of washing the schoolroom floor, and in this connection affecting much alarm for the children's health. A great controversy arose: ought the floor to be washed or ought it to be swept? Before long Maillebois was divided into two camps, which became quite impassioned and hurled all sorts of arguments at one another. The children's parents were consulted, and Savin, the clerk, denounced the washing system so bitterly that for a moment it was thought he would remove his twin boys from the school. But Marc carried the question to a higher court, soliciting the opinion of his superiors, and requesting them to appoint a commission of medical men and hygienists. Then came a serious investigation, and victory rested with the washing system. For the master this was quite a triumph; the children's parents became more and more disposed to support him; even Savin, with whom it was so difficult to deal, had to retract, and another boy came back from the Brothers' school, which, people began to say, was horribly dirty.

But, in spite of this dawning sympathy, Marc harboured no illusions. He felt that years would be necessary to free the region from the poison of Clericalism. Gaining a little more ground every now and then, he practised the greatest prudence, well pleased with the result, however slight it might be. At the instance of Geneviève, he had carried his desire for peace so far as to renew his intercourse with her relations. This, as it happened, took place in connection with the famous washing controversy, in which, contrary to custom, the ladies shared his views. So now, from time to time, accompanying his wife and daughter, he again visited the little house on the Place des Capucins. The two old ladies remained ceremonious and carefully avoided all dangerous subjects of conversation. Thus there was no pleasant intimacy. Nevertheless the reconciliation delighted Geneviève, for it freed her from the embarrassment she had felt when calling alone on her grandmother and mother. At present she saw them almost daily, and sometimes left Louise with them, coming and going from one house to the other, Marc evincing no anxiety, but feeling, indeed, well pleased with the gaiety displayed by his wife, on whom the ladies again lavished caresses, services, and little presents.

One Sunday, on going to lunch with a friend at Jonville, Marc—by the force of contrast—suddenly realised how much ground he had already gained at Maillebois. He had never previously understood how decisive a schoolmaster's influence might prove. Whilst Maillebois was slowly reverting to justice, health, and prosperity, he found Jonville relapsing into darkness, poverty, and stagnation. It grieved him to find that little or nothing remained of the good work he had done there in former years. And this was due solely to the deplorable action of the new schoolmaster, Jauffre, who cared for nothing save his own personal success. Short, dark, quick and cunning, with narrow prying eyes, Jauffre owed his success in life to the priest of his native village, who had taken him from his father, a blacksmith, to teach him his first lessons. Later on another priest had enriched him by negotiating his marriage with a butcher's daughter, who was short and dark like himself, and who brought him as dowry an income of two thousand francs a year. Jauffre was convinced, therefore, that if he desired to become a personage he ought to remain on the side of the priests, who some day doubtless would provide him with a splendid position. The income he owed to his wife already rendered him respectable, and his superiors treated him with consideration, for a man who was not dependent on the administration for his living could hardly be hustled about as if he were a mere starveling like Férou. In the school world, as elsewhere, favours go to the rich, never to the poor.

Besides, exaggerated reports were spread respecting Jauffre's fortune, in such wise that all the peasants took off their hats to him, he completing his conquest of them by his greed for gain, his wonderful skill in extracting as much profit as possible from everybody and everything. He was not troubled with any sincere belief; if he were a Republican, a good patriot, and a good Catholic, it was only so far as his interests required. Thus, although he called upon Abbé Cognasse as soon as he was appointed to Jonville, he did not immediately hand the school over to him, for he detected the anti-clerical spirit then prevalent in the village. But he gradually allowed the priest to become all-powerful by intentional relinquishment of his own privileges, and by covert resistance to the express desires of the Mayor and the parish council. Mayor Martineau, so strong and firm when he had leant on Marc, became quite lost on having to contend single-handed against the new schoolmaster, who soon became the real ruler of the parish, and ended by relinquishing his authority to Abbé Cognasse in such wise that, at the expiration of six months, Jonville was in the priest's hands.

Jauffre's line of conduct interested Marc particularly, because it was a masterpiece of Jesuitry. He obtained precise information about it from the schoolmistress, Mademoiselle Mazeline, on whom he called. She was sincerely grieved at being unable to effect anything useful now that she remained alone in a parish where all was rotting. She told Marc, of the comedy played by Jauffre in the earlier days when Mayor Martineau complained of one or another encroachment on the part of the priest, which the schoolmaster himself had stealthily provoked. The latter pretended to be as indignant as the Mayor, and accused his wife, Madame Jauffre, who was very devout, of assisting Abbé Cognasse. As it happened, the husband

and the wife were in full agreement, and had devised this plan in order to escape responsibility. And so Martineau was speedily vanquished, particularly as his coquettish wife became the great friend of Madame Jauffre, who, on the strength of her dower, affected the manners of a born lady. Before long Jauffre began to ring the bell for Mass, a duty which Marc had always refused to discharge. It brought in only thirty francs a year, but then, in Jauffre's opinion, thirty francs were not to be sneezed at. At Marc's instigation the money had been devoted for a time to the repair of the old church clock, and now the latter, being neglected as in former days, got out of order once more, in such wise that the peasants never again knew the correct time, for the clock went by fits and starts, being one day too fast and another too slow. As Mademoiselle Mazeline remarked, with a sad smile, that clock was the image of the parish, where nothing was now done in accordance with sense and logic.

The worst was that Abbé Cognasse's triumph extended to Le Moreux, whose Mayor, Saleur, the ex-grazier, impressed by the turn which things were taking at Jonville, and fearing for the fat life which he led, thanks to his new wealth, went back to the Church, however little he might really like the priests. And it was on that wretched rebel schoolmaster, Férou, that the effects of the reconciliation fell. Whenever Abbé Cognasse now came to Le Moreux, he displayed a most insolent sense of victory, and inflicted on the schoolmaster all sorts of humiliations, with which the other had to put up, abandoned as he was by the Mayor and the parish council. Never did a poor man lead a more rageful life. Possessed of a broad, quick mind, but condemned to live among so much ignorance and malice, Férou was impelled to the most extreme views by his ever-increasing misery. His wife, worn out by hard toil, and his three poor, pale, and puny daughters were starving. Yet, although indebtedness was consuming his last resources, he did not submit. Looking more of a scarecrow than ever in his old whitening frock coat, he evinced greater and greater bitterness, not only refusing to take his pupils to Mass, but even growling insults when the priest went by on Sundays. A catastrophe was imminent, dismissal was inevitable, and, to make matters worse, as the unlucky man had served only eight of his ten years as a teacher, he would be seized by the military authorities immediately after his dismissal. What would become of the mournful wife and little girls, when the husband, the father, should be lodged in some barracks?

On leaving Jonville that day, Marc and Mademoiselle Mazeline, who accompanied him as far as the railway station, passed the church at the moment when vespers were ending. Palmyre, Abbé Cognasse's terrible old servant, stood on the threshold, taking stock of those who showed themselves good Christians. Jauffre came out, and two of his pupils saluted him in military fashion, a mark of deference which he exacted, and which flattered his patriotic feelings. Then appeared Madame Jauffre and Madame Martineau, Martineau himself, and a stream of peasants of both sexes. Marc hastened his steps in order to avoid recognition and an impulse to express his grief aloud. He was struck by the fact that Jonville was less well kept than formerly; signs of abandonment, of a diminution of prosperity were already apparent. But then was not that the law? Did not intellectual poverty engender material poverty? Filth and vermin have invaded every country where Roman Catholicism has triumphed. Wherever it has passed it has proved a blast of death, striking the soil with sterility, casting men into idleness and imbecility, for it is the very negation of life, and it kills nations like a slow but deadly poison.

Marc felt relieved when, on the morrow, he once more found himself in his school at Maillebois among the children whose minds and hearts he was striving to awaken. Doubtless his work progressed very slowly, but the result achieved lent him the strength to persevere. Unfortunately, the parents of his boys gave him no help. His advance would have been more rapid if the lads had found in their homes some continuance of the principles inculcated during their school hours. But the contrary happened at times. In Achille and Philippe Savin, Marc detected the sullen, jealous bitterness of their father, and he could only endeavour to check their propensity for falsehood, slyness, and tale-bearing. Again, though the Doloirs were intelligent enough if they had only been minded to learn, they showed little real improvement. Auguste was very inattentive and quarrelsome, and Charles followed in his elder brother's footsteps. With Fernand Bongard the difficulty was different; he was exceptionally obtuse, and it was only with an incredible amount of trouble that one could make him understand and remember the slightest thing. Yet there was some improvement among the boys in their *ensemble* since Marc had brought them under a regimen of reason and truth.

Besides, the young man did not hope to change the world with one generation of schoolboys. The elementary master's task requires the greatest patience and abnegation; and Marc's one desire was to furnish an example by giving his whole life to the obscure work of preparing the future. If others would only perform their duty one might hope that in three or four generations a new liberating France might be created, such as might emancipate the world. And the young man was ambitious of no immediate reward, no personal success, though to his great delight he did receive a recompense for his efforts in the satisfaction which one of his pupils, little Sébastien Milhomme, gave him. That gentle and remarkably intelligent lad had become passionately attached to truth. Not only was he the first of his class, but he also displayed much sincerity and uprightness, at once boyishly and charmingly uncompromising in character. His schoolfellows often chose him as umpire in a difficulty, and when he had pronounced judgment he would not admit that any should free themselves from the effects of his decision. Marc always felt happy when he saw Sébastien at his desk, with his long and somewhat pensive face crowned by fair and curly hair, and lighted by fine blue eyes, which, fixed on the master with an ardent desire to learn, drank in every lesson. And it was not only Sébastien's rapid progress which won Marc's heart; he was still fonder of the boy on account of all the good and generous qualities which he divined in him. Indeed, Sébastien's was an exquisite little nature which Marc took pleasure in wakening, one of those child-natures in which all the florescence of noble thoughts and noble deeds was beginning to bud.

A painful scene occurred one day towards the close of the afternoon lessons. Fernand Bongard, whom others were fond of teasing on account of his dense stupidity, had discovered that the peak of his cap had been torn off. Forthwith he had burst into tears, declaring that his mother would surely beat him. Marc wished to discover the author of this malicious act, but all the boys laughingly denied their guilt, Auguste Doloir more impudently even than the others, though there was reason to suspect that the misdeed was his work. And, indeed, as it was proposed to keep the whole school in after lessons, until the culprit should confess, Achille Savin betrayed Auguste by pulling the peak of Fernand's cap out of his pocket. This gave Marc an opportunity to denounce falsehood, and he did so with so much warmth that the culprit himself shed tears and asked forgiveness. But Sébastien Milhomme's emotion was extraordinary, and when the others departed he lingered in the empty schoolroom, looking at his master with a desperate expression in his eyes.

'Have you something to say to me, my boy?' Marc asked him.

'Yes, monsieur,' Sébastien replied. Yet he became silent, his lips trembling, and his handsome face flushing with confusion.

'Is it very difficult to say, then?' Marc inquired.

'Yes, monsieur, it's a falsehood which I told you, and which makes me feel very unhappy.'

The young master smiled, anticipating some peccadillo, some childishly exaggerated scruple of conscience. 'Well, tell me the truth,' he said, 'it will relieve you.'

Another pause of some length followed. Signs of a fresh mental battle became apparent in Sébastien's limpid blue eyes and even on his pure lips. But at last the boy made up his mind and said: 'Well, monsieur, I told you a falsehood a long time ago, when I was quite little and ignorant—I told you a falsehood by saying what was not true, that I had never seen my cousin Victor with that writing copy—you remember, monsieur—the copy which people talked about so much. He had given it to me as he did not want to keep it himself, for he felt anxious about it as he had taken it from the Brothers'. And on that very day when I told you I did not remember anything about it, I had hidden it in a copybook of my own.'

Marc listened, thunderstruck. Once more the whole Simon case seemed to arise before him, emerging from its apparent slumber. But he did not wish the lad to see how deeply he was stirred by the unexpected shock, and so he asked him: 'Are you sure that you are not again mistaken? Did the copy bear the words "*Aimez vous les uns les autres*"?'

'Yes, monsieur.'

'And there was a paraph down below? I have taught you what a paraph is, have I not?'

'Yes, monsieur.'

For a moment Marc relapsed into silence. His heart was beating violently, he feared lest the cry which was rising to his lips might escape him. Then, wishing to make quite sure, he continued: 'But why did you keep silent till now, my lad? And what induced you to tell me the truth this evening?'

Sébastien, already relieved, looked his master straight in the face with an expression of charming candour. His delicate smile returned, and he explained the wakening of his conscience in the simplest way.

'Oh! if I did not tell you the truth sooner, monsieur, it was because I felt no need of doing so. I no longer remembered that I had told you a falsehood, it was so long ago. But one day, here, you explained to us how wrong it was to tell falsehoods, and then I remembered it, and began to feel worried. Afterwards, every time you spoke of the happiness one found in always saying the truth, I felt the more worried because I had not said it to you.... And to-day it pained me so I couldn't bear it any longer, and I had to tell you.'

Emotion brought tears to Marc's eyes. So his lessons were already flowering in that little mind, and it was he who garnered that first harvest—a harvest of truth—such precious truth, too, which would perhaps enable him to bring about a little justice. Never had he hoped for so prompt and so sweet a reward. The emotion he felt was exquisite. With an impulse of tender affection he stooped and kissed the lad.

'Thank you, my little Sébastien, you have given me great pleasure, and I love you with all my heart.'

Emotion had come upon the boy also. 'Oh! I love you very much, monsieur,' he answered, 'for otherwise I should not have dared to tell you everything.'

Marc resisted his desire to question the boy fully, for he feared lest he might be accused of having abused his authority as master to aggravate the confession. He merely ascertained that Madame Alexandre had taken the copy-slip from her son, who did not know what she had done with it, for she had never again mentioned it to him. For the rest, the young man preferred to see the mother. She alone could produce the slip—if it were still in her possession—and what a precious document it would prove, for would it not constitute the long-sought 'new fact,' which might enable Simon's family to apply for the revision of his iniquitous trial?

On remaining alone, Marc felt full of joy. He wished it were possible for him to hasten to the Lehmanns immediately, to tell them the good news, and impart a little happiness to their sad, mourning home, which was the object of so much popular execration. At last! at last! a sunray had flashed upon the black night of iniquity.

Going upstairs to join his wife, he cried to her as he reached the threshold, such was his excitement, his craving to relieve his heart: 'Geneviève, do you know, I now have proof of Simon's innocence ... Ah! justice is wakening; we shall be able to go forward now!'

He had not noticed the presence, in a shadowy corner, of Madame Duparque, who, since the reconciliation, condescended to visit her granddaughter occasionally. She, on hearing him, gave a start and exclaimed in her harsh voice: 'What? Simon's innocence! Do you still persevere in your folly, then? A proof indeed! What proof do you mean?'

Then, after he had related his conversation with little Milhomme, the old lady again flew into a temper: 'The evidence of a child! That isn't of much value! He now pretends that he formerly lied; but what proof is there that he is not lying now?... So the culprit would be a Brother, eh? Oh! speak your mind plainly, acknowledge it; your only object is to accuse one of the Brothers, is that not so? It is always the same rageful impiety with you!'

Somewhat disconcerted at having thus come upon the old lady, and wishing to spare his wife the grief of any fresh rupture, Marc contented himself with saying: 'I won't discuss things with you, grandmother. I merely wished to inform Geneviève of some news which was likely to please her.'

'But your news does not please her!' cried Madame Duparque. 'Look at her!'

Marc turned towards his wife, who stood there in the fading light which fell from the window. And indeed, to his surprise, he saw that she was grave, that her beautiful eyes had darkened, as if the night, now slowly approaching, had filled them with shadows.

'Is it true, Geneviève?' he asked her; 'does a work of justice no longer please you?'

She did not answer him at once. She had become pale and embarrassed, as if tortured by painful hesitation. And just as he, likewise feeling very uneasy, was repeating his question, she was saved the distress of answering him by the sudden appearance of Madame Alexandre.

Sébastien, on returning home, had bravely told his mother of his confession respecting the copy-slip. She had lacked the strength to scold him for his good action; but full of fear at the thought that the schoolmaster would call, question her, and demand the document in the presence of her terrible sister-in-law, Madame Edouard, who was so anxious for the prosperity of their little stationery business, she had preferred to go to the school and do what she could to bury the affair at once.

Yet now she was there her discomfort became great indeed. Like a gust of wind she had darted out of her shop, hardly knowing what she would say, and at present she remained stammering, full of embarrassment, particularly as she perceived Geneviève and Madame Duparque with Marc, whom she had hoped to see privately, alone.

'Monsieur Froment,' she began, 'Sébastien has just told me, yes, of that confession he thought fit to make to you.... So I deemed it best to give you the reasons of my conduct. You understand—do you not?—all the worry which such a story would bring us with the difficulties that already beset us in our business. Well, the fact is, it's true; I did have that paper, but it no longer exists; I destroyed it.'

She breathed again as if relieved, having contrived to say what she considered necessary in order to be freed from trouble.

'You destroyed it!' Marc exclaimed with a pang. 'Oh! Madame Alexandre!'

Some slight embarrassment returned to her and she once more sought her words: 'I did wrong, perhaps.... But think of our position! We are two poor women with nobody to assist us. And, besides, it was so sad to have our children mixed up in that abominable affair.... I could not keep a paper which prevented me from sleeping: I burnt it....'

She was still quivering so perceptibly that Marc looked at her as she stood there, tall and fair, with the gentle face of a woman of loving nature. And it seemed to him that she was experiencing some secret torment. For a moment he felt suspicious—wondered if she were lying—and it occurred to him to test her sincerity.

'By destroying that paper, Madame Alexandre,' he said, 'you condemned an innocent man a second time.... Think of all that he is suffering yonder. You would weep if I read his letters to you. There can be no worse torture than his—the deadly climate, the harshness of his keepers, and, above all else, the consciousness of his innocence and the fearful obscurity as to the truth, amid which he is struggling.... And And what a frightful nightmare for you, should you remember that all this is your work!'

She had become quite white, and her hands moved involuntarily as if to ward off some horrible vision. There was kindness and weakness in her nature, but Marc could not tell whether it were a quiver of remorse, or some desperate struggle that he detected in her. For a moment, as if imploring help, she stammered wildly: 'My poor child! my poor child!'

And that child, that little Sébastien, to whom she was so fondly, so passionately attached, to whom she would have sacrificed everything, must have suddenly appeared before her, and have restored some little of her strength. 'Oh! you are cruel, Monsieur Froment!' she said; 'you make me terribly unhappy.... But how can it be helped, since it's done? I cannot find that paper again among the ashes.'

'So you burnt it, Madame Alexandre—you are sure of it?'

'Certainly, I told you so.... I burnt it for fear lest my little man should be compromised, and suffer from it all his life.'

She spoke those last words in an ardent voice, as if with fierce resolution. Marc was convinced, and made a gesture of despair. Once again the triumph of truth was delayed, prevented. Without a word he escorted Madame Alexandre to the door, she again becoming all embarrassment, at a loss indeed how to take leave of the ladies who were present. Bowing and stammering excuses, she disappeared, and, when she was gone, deep silence reigned in the room.

Neither Geneviève nor Madame Duparque had intervened. Both had remained frigid and motionless. And they still preserved silence while Marc, absorbed in his grief, his head bowed, walked slowly to and fro.

At last, however, Madame Duparque rose to take her departure, and on reaching the threshold she turned and said: 'That woman is a lunatic! Her story of a destroyed paper appears to me to be a fairy tale which nobody would believe. You would do wrong to relate it, for it would not help on your affairs.... Good-night: be sensible.'

Marc did not even answer. With a heavy tread he long continued walking up and down. Night had gathered round, and Geneviève lighted the lamp. And when by its pale glow she began to lay the table in silence, her husband did not even try to confess her. One sorrow was enough, and he did not wish to hasten the advent of another, such as would come should he learn, as he might, that she, his wife, was no longer in communion with him in respect to many things.

But during the following days he was haunted by Madame Duparque's last words. Supposing indeed that he should try to make use of the new fact which had come to his knowledge, what credit would his statement obtain among the public? Doubtless he would secure the testimony of Sébastien; the boy would repeat that he had seen the copy-slip which his cousin Victor had brought from the Brothers' school. But it would be the testimony of a child barely ten years old, and his mother would strive to weaken its importance. It was the paper itself that ought to be produced; and the statement that it had been burnt would merely lead to the affair being buried once again.

The more Marc reflected, the more he understood the necessity of waiting. The new fact could not be put to use, given the conditions in which he had discovered it. And yet for him how precious it was, how fertile in decisive proof! It rendered his faith in Simon's innocence unshakable, it confirmed all his deductions, materialised the conviction to which reasoning had brought him. One of the Brothers was the real culprit; a legally conducted inquiry would soon have shown which of them it was. Yet the young man again had to resign himself to patience, and rely on the strength of truth, which was now at last on the march, and which would never more be stopped until full light should be cast upon everything.

At the same time Marc's anguish increased, the torture of his conscience became more tragical day by day. It was frightful to know that an innocent man was suffering abominable martyrdom in a penal settlement, and that the real culprit was free, near at hand, impudent and triumphant, still pursuing his vile work as a corrupter of children; and it was still more frightful that one should be unable to cry all that aloud and prove it, confronted as one was by the base complicity of all the social forces banded together by egotistical interest to perpetuate the monstrous iniquity. Marc no longer slept, he carried his secret with him like a sharp goad which incessantly reminded him that it was his duty to ensure justice. Never for an hour did he cease to think of his mission, and his heart bled despairingly because he knew not what to do to hasten its success.

Even at the Lehmanns he said nothing of Sébastien's confession. What good would it have done to give these poor folk a vague uncertain hope? Life still treated them very harshly, overwhelmed them with opprobrium and grief—grief for the prisoner yonder, whose letters rent their hearts, and whose name was cast in their teeth as a supreme insult. Old Lehmann's trade had declined yet more; Rachel, always gowned in mourning like a widow, distressed by the rapid growth of her children, who would learn everything before long, scarcely dared to go out. Thus Marc only confided in David, in whom glowed the stubborn determination to make everybody recognise and acclaim his brother's innocence at some future time. He lived apart, ignored, carefully avoiding all appearance on the scene, but never, not for an hour, did he pause in the task of rehabilitation which had become the sole object of his life. He reflected, studied, followed clues which he too often had to abandon after a few steps. Despite two years of constant research, he had discovered nothing decisive. His suspicion of an illegal communication made by President Gragnon to the jurors had become a moral certainty, only he had failed in all his efforts to procure proof, and could not tell how to obtain it. Nevertheless he was not discouraged; he had resolved to devote ten, twenty years of his life even, to reach the real culprit. Marc's revelation inspired him with additional courage and patience. He likewise held that it was best to keep Sébastien's confession secret, so long as it was not strengthened by some material proof. For the moment it merely supplied the hope of an additional triumph. And that said, David again turned, calmly and firmly, to his investigations, pursuing them with no haste, but ever in the same prudent, continuous manner.

One morning, before lessons began, Marc at last made up his mind to remove the large crucifix which hitherto he had left hanging from the wall behind his desk. He had been waiting for two years to be sufficiently master of the situation before expressing in this manner the independence of the secular school—such as he understood and desired it—in matters of religion. Until now he had willingly yielded to Salvan's prudent advice, for he understood that he must assure himself of his position before making it a position of combat. But he now felt strong enough to begin the battle. Had he not restored prosperity to the Communal school by winning back to it numerous pupils who had been transferred to the Brothers'? Had he not gradually gained personal respect, the affection of the children, the favour of their parents? Besides, he was impelled to take action first by his recent visit to Jonville, which he had left on the high road to knowledge, and which Abbé Cognasse was once more transforming into an abode of darkness, and secondly by all the anxiety and anger stirred up within him by Sébastien's confession—anger with the ignominy that he divined around him in Maillebois, which was enslaved and poisoned by the clerical faction.

That morning, then, he had already climbed upon a stool to remove the crucifix, when Geneviève, holding little Louise by the hand, entered the classroom to inform him of her intention to take the child to spend the day with her grandmother. At the sight of Marc on the stool the young woman was quite surprised. 'What are you doing there?' she asked him.

'Can't you see?' he answered. 'I am taking down this crucifix, which I intend to give to Abbé Quandieu myself, in order that he may restore it to the church which it ought never to have left.... Here! help me—take it!'

But she did not hold out her arms. She did not move. Turning extremely pale, she watched him as if she were witnessing some forbidden and dangerous deed which filled her with fear. And he had to descend from the stool unhelped by her, encumbered with the big crucifix, which he immediately locked up in one of the cupboards.

'You wouldn't help me,' he exclaimed. 'What is the matter? Do you disapprove of what I have done?'

In spite of her emotion, Geneviève answered plainly: 'Yes, I disapprove of it.'

Her answer amazed Marc. Like her he began to quiver. It was the first time that she assumed such an aggressive and angry tone with him. He felt a little shock, a slight rending, such as presages rupture. And he looked at her with astonishment and anxiety, as if he had heard a voice he did not know, as if a stranger had just spoken to him.

'What! you disapprove of what I do? Was it really you who said that?'

'Yes, it was I. It is wrong of you to do what you have done.'

She it was indeed; for she stood before him, tall and slender, with her fair amiable face, and her glance gleaming with some of her father's sensual passion. Yes, it was she, and yet in the expression of those large blue eyes there was already something different, a shadow, a little of the mystical dimness of the *au-delà*. And Marc in his astonishment felt a chill come to his heart as he suddenly observed that change. What had happened, then? Why was she no longer the same? But he recoiled from an immediate explanation, and contented himself with adding: 'Hitherto, even when you did not think perhaps as I did, you always told me to act in accordance with my conscience, and that is what I have now done. And so your blame surprised me painfully. We shall have to talk of it.'

She did not disarm, she preserved her angry frigidity of manner. 'We will talk of it if you so desire,' she replied; 'meantime I am going to take Louise to grandmother, who will not bring her back till this evening.'

Sudden enlightenment dawned upon Marc. It was Madame Duparque who was taking Geneviève from him, and who, doubtless, would take Louise also. He had acted wrongly in disinteresting himself from his wife's doings, in allowing her and the child to spend so much time in that pious house, where the dimness and atmosphere of a chapel prevailed. He had failed to notice the stealthy change which had been taking place in his wife during the last two years, that revival of her pious youth, of the indelible education of other days, which, little by little, had been bringing her back to the dogmas which he imagined had been overcome by the efforts of his intellect and the embrace of his love. As yet she had not begun to follow her religion again by attendance at Mass, Communion, and Confession, but he felt that she was already parting from him, reverting to the past with slow but certain steps, each of which would place them farther and farther asunder.

'Are we no longer in agreement, then, my darling?' he asked her sadly.

With great frankness she replied: 'No. And grandmother was right, Marc; all the trouble has come from that horrible affair. Since you have been defending that man, who was transported and who deserved his punishment, misfortune has entered our home, and we shall end by agreeing no more in anything.'

He raised a cry of despair. 'Is it you,' he repeated, 'you who speak like that? You are against truth, against justice now!'

'I am against the deluded and malicious ones whose evil passions attack religion. They wish to destroy God; but, even if one quits the Church, one should at least respect its ministers, who do so much good.'

This time Marc made no rejoinder. A quarrel was out of place at that moment when he was expecting the arrival of the boys. But was the evil so deep already? His grief arose chiefly from the fact that at the root of the dissentiment parting him from his wife he found the Simon affair, the mission of equity which he had imposed on himself. No concession in that matter was possible on his part, and thus no agreement could be arrived at. For two years past that monstrous affair had been mingled with every incident; it was like a poisoned source which would continue to rot both people and things, so long as justice was not done. And now his own home was poisoned by it.

Seeing that he preserved silence, Geneviève went towards the door, repeating quietly: 'Well, I am going to grandmother's with Louise.'

Marc thereupon caught up the child as if anxious to kiss her. Would he also allow that little one, the flesh of his flesh, to be taken from him? Ought he not to keep her in his arms to save her from imbecile and deadly contagion? For a moment he looked at her. Already at five years of age, she showed signs of becoming tall and slender like her mother, her grandmother, and her great-grandmother. But she lacked their pale fair hair, and she had the lofty brow of the Froments, the brow that suggested an impregnable tower of sense and knowledge. Laughing loudly, she cast her arms prettily about her father's neck.

'You know, papa, I will repeat my fable to you when I come home; I know it quite well.'

Yielding to a sentiment of tolerance, Marc, for the second time, resolved that he would have no dispute. He restored the little one to her mother, who led her away. Moreover, the boys were now arriving, and the classroom soon became full. But anxiety remained in the master's heart at the thought of the struggle which he had resolved to wage when he removed the crucifix from the wall. That struggle, it was now certain, would reach his own hearth. His tears and the tears of his loved ones would flow. Nevertheless, by an heroic effort, he mastered his suffering; and summoning little Sébastien, the monitor, he bade him watch over the reading class, while for his part he gaily proceeded with some demonstrations on the blackboard, amidst the joyous brightness with which the sunshine flooded the schoolroom.

CHAPTER II

Three days later, in the evening, while Marc was undressing in the bedroom, Geneviève being already in bed, he told her that he had received an urgent letter from Salvan, who wished to see him on the morrow, Sunday.

'No doubt it is about that crucifix which I removed from the classroom,' the young man added. 'Some parents have complained, it seems; and very likely there will be a great to-do. But I anticipated it.'

Geneviève, whose head lay deep in her pillow, returned no answer. But when Marc was in bed and the light was extinguished, he was delightfully surprised to find her casting her arms about him, and whispering in his ear: 'I spoke to you harshly the other day; and, it's true, I don't think as you do about religion or about the affair; but I still love you very dearly, I love you with all my heart.'

Marc felt the more moved by these words as, since the recent dispute, his wife had turned her back upon him, as though in token of conjugal rupture.

'And as you are going to have trouble,' she continued softly, 'I don't want you to think me angry. One's ideas may differ, but all the same one may love one another very much—is it not so? And if you are mine, I am still yours, my dear, dear husband.'

On hearing her speak like that he clasped her to him with passionate eagerness. 'Ah! my dear wife, as long as you love me, as long as you are mine,' said he, 'I shall fear nought of the terrible threats around us.'

She yielded to his embrace, quivering, transported by the joy of love which was essential to her being. And there came a moment of perfect communion, irresistible reconciliation. The good understanding of a young couple, united by love, is only seriously threatened when some divergency of that love arises. As long as they are swayed by passion one for the other, they remain in agreement athwart the worst mishaps. He who would part them must first of all destroy their mutual passion.

When Marc gave Geneviève a last kiss before both fell asleep, he thought it well to reassure her: 'I shall act very prudently in this affair, I promise you,' said he. 'You know too that I am moderate and reasonable at bottom.'

'Ah! do as you please,' she answered prettily. 'All I ask is that you should come back to me, and that we should still love each other.'

On the morrow the young man repaired to Beaumont, quite enlivened by his wife's ardent affection. He derived fresh courage from it, and thus it was with a smiling face and the demeanour of a combatant that he entered Salvan's private room at the Training College. But the first words spoken by the director, after they had shaken hands in a friendly way, surprised and embarrassed him.

'I say, my good fellow,' Salvan began, 'so it seems that you have at last discovered the new fact, the long-sought proof of our poor Simon's innocence, which will enable one to apply for the revision of his trial?'

Marc, who had anticipated an immediate explanation on the subject of the crucifix, remained for a moment silent, wondering whether he ought to tell the truth even to Salvan. At last, seeking his words, he said slowly: 'The new fact ... no, I have nothing decisive as yet.'

But Salvan did not notice his hesitation. 'That is what I thought,' he rejoined, 'for you would have warned me, eh? Nevertheless, there is a rumour of some discovery made by you, a document of capital importance, placed in your hands by chance, something like a sword of Damocles which you are said to hold over the heads of the real culprit and his accomplices, the whole clerical gang of the region.'

Marc listened, full of stupefaction. Who could have spoken? How was it that Sébastien's confession and his mother's visit had become known? How was it that particulars had been spread abroad, modified and exaggerated as they passed from mouth to mouth? The young man suddenly made up his mind to tell the truth to Salvan; he felt it necessary to confide in that worthy and sensible friend and adviser, on whom he placed so much reliance. So he told him how he knew that a copy-slip, similar to the one brought forward in evidence against Simon, had been taken from the Brothers' school, and how it had been destroyed.

Salvan, who was deeply moved, rose from his chair. 'It was the proof we needed!' he exclaimed. 'But you act rightly in remaining silent since we hold no material evidence. One must wait.... At present, however, I understand the disquietude, the covert alarm, which for some days past I have detected among our adversaries. Some words may have escaped you or the boy, or his mother, and chance words often go far; or else some mysterious agency may have placed the secret in circulation, misrepresenting the facts. In any case the culprit and his accomplices have certainly felt the ground quaking beneath them; and, naturally, they are alarmed, for they will have to defend their crime.'

Then, passing to the subject which had prompted his urgent letter, he resumed: 'But I wished to speak to you of another incident, which everybody is talking about—your removal of that crucifix from your classroom. You know my views: our schools ought to be purely and simply secular, therefore all religious symbols are out of place in them. But you can have no idea of the tempest which your action will raise. Unfortunately, it is now the interest of the good Brothers and their supporters, the Jesuits, to ruin you absolutely, alarmed as they are by the weapons which they believe to be in your hands. By your action in the matter of the crucifix you have laid yourself open to attack, and so they are naturally rushing forward to the onslaught.'

Marc understood, and made a gesture of defiance, like a man fully prepared for battle. 'But have I not acted prudently, in accordance with your advice?' he responded. 'Did I not wait two long years before removing that cross which was hung up after Simon's trial to indicate that the clerical faction had virtually taken possession of the Communal school? I have set that poor school on its legs again; it was suspected and discredited, and I have made it prosperous and free. So was it not legitimate that my first independent act as schoolmaster, after winning acceptance and then victory, should be to rid the school of all emblems, and restore it to that neutrality in matters of religion, from which it ought never to have departed?'

Salvan interrupted him: 'Once again, I do not blame you. You showed great patience and tolerance. Nevertheless, your action has taken place at a terrible moment, and, feeling alarmed for you, I wished to discuss matters in order to provide, if possible, for all dangerous contingencies.'

They sat down and talked at length. The political situation of the department was still very bad. Fresh elections had taken place recently, and the result had been another step in the direction of clerical reaction. An extraordinary thing had happened: Lemarrois, the Mayor of Beaumont, Gambetta's former friend, whose position as deputy had been deemed unassailable, had found himself obliged to submit to a second ballot, [1] through the advent of a Socialist candidate, none other than Advocate Delbos, whose address at Simon's trial had marked him out for the support of the revolutionary *faubourgs*; and, at the second polling, Lemarrois had only won by a majority of about a thousand votes. Meanwhile, the Royalist and Catholic reactionaries had gained a seat, the handsome Hector de Sanglebœuf having secured the return of a friend, a general officer, thanks to the entertainments which he gave at La Désirade, and the lavish manner in which he distributed Jew gold, derived from his father-in-law, Baron Nathan. Then, too, in order to secure re-election, the amiable Marcilly, once the hope of all the young men of culture, had skilfully completed his evolution towards the welcoming Church, which was very desirous of concluding a new pact with the *bourgeoisie*, whom the progress of Socialism terrified.

> [1] In French elections, when several nominees contest some particular seat, a candidate, to be successful, must obtain one half, *plus* one, of the total number of votes recorded. If no candidate secures that number a second ballot ensues a fortnight later. On the second occasion a relative majority suffices for election.—*Trans.*

Though it had accepted political equality the *bourgeoisie* indeed was unwilling to concede equality in the economic field, for it desired to restore nothing of what it had stolen. And to resist the onslaught from below, it preferred to ally itself with its old enemies. It again began to think that religion had some good features, that it was useful as a kind of police institution, a barrier, which alone might check the growing appetite of the masses. And as a first step the *bourgeoisie* was gradually garbing itself in militarism, nationalism, anti-semitism, and all the other hypocritical disguises under which invading Clericalism pursued its road.

The army became merely the emblem of brute force upholding the thefts of ages, an impregnable wall of bayonets within whose shelter property and capital, duly gorged, might digest in security. The nation, the country, was the *ensemble* of abuses and iniquities which it was criminal to touch, the monstrous social edifice, not one beam of which must be changed for dread lest all should fall. The Jews, even as in the Middle Ages, served as a pretext to instil fresh warmth into cooling beliefs, to exploit ancestral hatred, and sow the horrid seeds of civil war. And beneath that all-embracing movement of reaction there was nought save the stealthy labour of the Church, seeking to regain the ground she had formerly lost when the old world broke up beneath the liberating breath of the French Revolution. It was the Revolution that the Church strove to kill by regaining ascendency over the *bourgeoisie*, which the Revolution had raised to power, and which had decided to betray it in order to retain that power, of which it owed account to the masses. And the return of the *bourgeoisie* to the bosom of the Church would lead to the reconquest of the people, for the Church's vast design was to subjugate men by the influence of women, and particularly to lay hold of the children in their schools and confine their minds in the dim prison of dogmas. If the France of Voltaire were again becoming the France of Rome it was because the teaching Congregations had set their grip on the young. And the position was becoming worse and worse, the Church was already shrieking victory—victory over the democracy, victory over science—full of the hope that she would prevent the inevitable, the completion of the Revolution, the junction of the masses with the *bourgeoisie* in the seat of power, and the final liberation of the entire people.

'The situation grows worse daily,' said Salvan; 'you know what a frantic campaign is being carried on against our system of elementary education. Last Sunday, at Beaumont, a priest went so far as to say in the pulpit that a secular schoolmaster was Satan disguised as a pedagogue. "Fathers and mothers!" he cried, "you should wish your children to be dead rather than in such hells as those schools!"... As for secondary education, that also is a prey to clerical reaction. Apart from the ever-increasing prosperity of such Congregational establishments as the College of Valmarie, where the Jesuits finish poisoning the sons of the *bourgeoisie*, the officers, functionaries, and magistrates of the future, our Lycées, even, remain in the power of the priests. Here at Beaumont, for instance, the director, the devout Depinvilliers, openly receives Father Crabot, who is, I think, the confessor of his wife and daughters. Lately, as he felt discontented with Abbé Leriche, a worthy but very aged man who had fallen asleep in his post, he secured a thoroughly militant chaplain. At the Lycées, no doubt, religious exercises are optional; but for a boy to be exempted from them a request from his parents is required. And naturally the pupil about whom a fuss is made in that respect is badly noted, set upon one side, and even subjected to all sorts of petty persecutions.... Briefly, after thirty years of Republican rule, a century of active free thought, the Church still trains and educates our children, still remains paramount, intent on retaining her domination over the world by moulding in the same old moulds as formerly the men of bondage and error that she needs to govern on her behalf. And all the wretchedness of the times comes from that cause.'

'But what do you advise me to do, my friend?' Marc inquired. 'After acting as I have done, am I to retreat?'

'No, certainly not. Perhaps, if you had warned me, I might have begged you to wait a little longer. But as you have removed that crucifix you must defend yourself. After writing to you I saw Le Barazer, our Academy Inspector, and I now feel somewhat easier in mind. You know him, and you are aware how difficult it is to guess his thoughts. Yet I believe that he is at heart on our side, and I should be greatly surprised if he were to play into the hands of our enemies. But everything will depend on you, on your power of resistance, on the firmness of the position you have acquired at Maillebois. I foresee a frantic campaign on the part of the Brothers, the Capuchins, and the Jesuits, for you are not merely a secular schoolmaster, otherwise an incarnation of Satan, but you are, particularly, the defender of Simon—that is, the torchbearer, the soldier of truth and justice, whose light must be extinguished and whose lips must be sealed. In any case, be prudent and sensible and keep up your courage.'

Salvan, who had risen, grasped the young man's hands, and for a moment they remained thus, smiling as they gazed at each other, their eyes shining with courage and faith.

'At least you do not despair of the final result, my friend?'

'Despair, my boy? Ah! never! Victory is certain; I do not know when it will come, but it is certain. Besides, there is more cowardice and egotism than actual malice among some of our adversaries. How many of our university men are neither really good nor really bad, though on striking an average one finds perhaps rather more goodness than evil among them. The worst is that they are functionaries, and as such are wedded to routine, apart from which their one concern is their advancement, as is natural. Forbes, our Rector, harbours, I fancy, the contempt of a philosopher for these wretched times, and on that account is content to play the part of a piece of administrative mechanism connecting the Minister with the university staff. Then, too, if Depinvilliers sets himself on the side of the Church, it is merely because he has two ugly daughters on his hands, and relies on Father Crabot to supply them with rich husbands. As for the terrible Mauraisin—whom you will do well to beware of, for he has an ugly soul—he would like to be in my shoes; and he would go over to your side to-morrow if he thought you in a position to give him my berth.... Yes, yes, many of them are merely poor hungry devils, while others are men of weak intellect—they will come over to our side and even help us when we have won the battle.'

He laughed indulgently. Then, becoming grave once more, he added: 'Besides, the good work I do here prevents me from despairing. As you know, I hide myself away in my little corner; but, day by day, I strive to hasten the future. And things move—they move. I am very well satisfied with my young men. No doubt it is still rather difficult to recruit students, for the profession appears so thankless, so poorly paid, leading to nothing but contumely and a life of certain wretchedness. All the same, we had more competitors than usual this year. It is hoped that the Chambers will end by voting reasonable salaries, such as may enable the humblest masters to live in some little dignity. And you will see, you will see what will happen when properly trained masters leave this college and spread through the villages and the towns, carrying words of deliverance with them, destroying error, superstition, and falsehood on all sides, like the missionaries of a new humanity! The Church will be vanquished then, for it can only subsist and triumph amid ignorance, and when it is swept away the whole nation will march unchecked towards solidarity and peace.'

'Ah! my old friend, that is the great hope!' cried Marc; 'that is what lends all of us the strength and cheerfulness we need to do our work. Thanks for inspiriting me; I will try to be sensible and courageous.'

They once more shook hands energetically, and Marc returned to Maillebois, where the fiercest battle, war to the knife, awaited him.

There, as at Beaumont, the political situation had become worse. The last municipal elections, following those for the Chamber of Deputies, had also given disastrous results. Darras had found his party in a minority in the new Municipal Council; and Philis, the clerical councillor, the leader of the reactionary cause, had now been elected Mayor. Before everything else, Marc wished to see Darras in order to ascertain how far the latter might yet be able to support him. So he presented himself, one evening, in the comfortable drawing-room of the handsome house which the contractor had built himself. Darras, as soon as he perceived him, raised his arms to the ceiling.

'Ah! my dear schoolmaster, so now you have the whole pack at your heels! Oh! I shall be on your side, you may rely on me now that I am beaten, reduced to opposition.... It was difficult for me to be always on your side when I was Mayor; for, as you know, the majority I disposed of was only one of two votes. But even when I had to act contrary to your desires, I repeated to myself that you were a thousand times right. At present we shall be able to go forward, since the only course open to me is to fight and try to upset Philis, and take the mayoralty from him. You did quite right when you removed that crucifix from the schoolroom; it wasn't there in Simon's time, and it ought never to have been there at all.'

Marc made bold to smile. 'Why, every time I spoke to you of removing it,' said he, 'you protested. You talked of the necessity of prudence, of the danger of frightening the children's parents, and giving our adversaries a weapon against us.'

'But I have just admitted to you how embarrassed I was! Ah! it is by no means easy to manage a town like Maillebois, where the forces of the different parties have always balanced, and where nobody has ever been able to tell whether the freethinkers or the priests would win the day. At this moment we are certainly not in a brilliant position, but we must keep up our courage. We shall end by giving them a good licking, which will make us masters of the town for good.'

'That's certain,' replied Marc, delighted with the fine valour displayed by the ambitious contractor, who, at heart, was a worthy man.

'Particularly,' continued Darras, 'as Philis won't dare to take any serious step, for, in his turn, he has only a majority of two, such as rendered me so timid. He is condemned to mark time, and will live in constant fear of some slight change which may place him in a minority. I know by experience what that means!'

He made merry over it in a noisy way. He harboured against Philis the hatred of a big and healthy man with a sound stomach and a sound brain, who was chagrined by the sight of the new Mayor's lean little figure, dark, hard face, pointed nose and thin lips. Philis had retired from business as a tilt and awning maker, at the time of his wife's death, and, though possessed of an income of some ten thousand francs a year, the real origin of which remained somewhat obscure, he lived in great retirement, attended by a single servant, a huge fair creature of whom evil tongues spoke very badly. Her master had a daughter named Octavie, twelve years of age, now with the nuns of the Visitation at Beaumont, and a son, Raymond, ten years old, who was a boarder at the Jesuit College of Valmarie, pending the time when he might enter the military school of St. Cyr. Having thus rid himself of his children, the new Mayor led a close, narrow life, most careful in all his religious observances, ever in conference with the black frocks, and really acting as the executor of the Congregations' decisions. His election as Mayor was sufficient proof of the acute stage which the religious crisis had reached in that town of Maillebois, which the struggle between the Republic and the Church was ravaging.

'And so I may go forward,' said Marc; 'you will support me with the minority of the Council?'

'Why, certainly!' cried Darras. 'Only, be reasonable, don't give us too big an affair to deal with.'

On the very morrow the contest began; and apparently it was Savin, the clerk, the father of the twin boys, Achille and Philippe, who was chosen to strike the first blow. At all events, on leaving his office in the evening, he came to the school to pick a quarrel with the master.

'You know what I am—is that not so, Monsieur Froment?' said he. 'I am a radical Republican, and nobody can suspect me of conspiring with the priests. Nevertheless, on behalf of a number of parents I have come to ask you to replace that crucifix which you removed, for religion is necessary for children as well as for women.... No priests in the school, I agree to that; but Christ, remember it, was the first of Republicans and revolutionaries!'

Marc, however, desired to know the names of the other parents whom Savin represented. 'If you have not come merely on your own behalf,' said he, 'will you tell me what families have delegated you?'

'Oh! "delegated"—that is not quite correct. I have seen Doloir the mason, and Bongard the farmer, and have found that they blame you as I myself do. Only, it is always compromising to protest and give one's signature—is that not so? I myself risk a good deal by coming forward, on account of my superiors. But the voice of my conscience as the father of a family speaks too loudly for me to act otherwise. How shall I ever manage those two scapegraces of mine, Achille and Philippe, if you do not frighten them a little with fear of the punishment of God and the torments of hell? Look at my big girl, Hortense, who is so good in every respect, and who was admired by all Maillebois when she took her first Communion this year! By taking her to church, Mademoiselle Rouzaire has made her really perfect. Compare your work with Mademoiselle Rouzaire's, compare my two boys with my daughter. By that comparison alone you stand condemned, Monsieur Froment.'

Marc smiled in his quiet way. The amiable Hortense, a pretty and precocious girl of thirteen, one of Mademoiselle Rouzaire's favourites, occasionally contrived to climb over the wall separating the playgrounds of the two schools, in order that she might hide away in corners with lads of her own age. Even as Savin had suggested, the young man had often compared his pupils, from whom by degrees he obtained a little more reason and truth, with the pupils of the schoolmistress, his neighbour—the affectedly prim and gentle little girls who were fed on clerical pap, falsehood, and hypocrisy, and perturbed, even secretly spoilt, by the corrupting influence of the mysterious. Marc would have liked to have seen his boys and those girls together—those girls who were now reared and educated apart, from whom everything was hidden, whose minds and whose senses were heated by all the fires of mysticism. They would then have ceased to climb over walls to go in search of so-called sin, the forbidden fruit of damnation and delight. Yes, only a system of mixed schools could ensure the health and strength of the free and happy nation of to-morrow. [2]

> [2] This problem seems to have been solved in the United States, where, judging by official reports, the mingling of the sexes in the schools is extensive. Thence (I judge the matter as an European) must have come the very great and distinctly beneficial influence exercised by American women on the national character. Perhaps it is not too much to say that, apart from such incentives as a mere desire to gain money, the women of the United States have largely helped to make their race the most enterprising and progressive in the world. As for the influence of mixed

schools on morals, Americans have repeatedly assured me that it has been the best possible.—*Trans.*

To Savin, however, Marc merely said: 'Mademoiselle Rouzaire does her duty as she understands it; and I do mine in the same way.... If families would only help me, the good work of training and education would progress more rapidly.'

At this Savin lost his temper. Lean and puny, buttoned up in his shabby frock coat, he drew himself erect on his little legs: 'Do you insinuate that I give bad examples to my children?' he asked.

'Oh! certainly not. Only everything that I teach them here is afterwards contradicted by what they see in the world around them. They find truthfulness regarded as dangerous audacity, and reason condemned as being insufficient, incapable of forming honest men.'

Marc indeed was greatly grieved that he should be thwarted so often by his pupils' parents, when he dreamt of obtaining from them the necessary help to hasten the emancipation of the humble. If on leaving school every day the children had only found in their homes some realisation of their lessons, some practice of the social duties and rights in which they were instructed, how much easier and swifter would have been the march of improvement! Such collaboration was even indispensable; the schoolmaster could not suffice for many things, the most delicate, the most useful, when his pupils' parents did not continue his work in the same spirit and complete it. The master and the parents ought to have gone hand in hand towards the same goal of truth and justice. And how sad it was when, instead of obtaining the parents' help, the master saw them destroying the little good he effected, unconscious for the most part of what they were doing, yielding simply to the incoherence of their ideas and their lives.

But Savin was again speaking. 'Briefly,' said he, 'you will hang up that cross again, Monsieur Froment, if you wish to please us all, and live on good terms with us, which is what we desire, for you are not a bad schoolmaster.'

Marc smiled again. 'Thank you,' he said. 'But why did not Madame Savin accompany you? She, at any rate, would have been playing her proper part, for she follows the observances of the Church—I know it.'

'She is religious, as all respectable women ought to be,' the clerk answered dryly. 'I would rather have her go to Mass than take a lover.'

He looked at Marc suspiciously, consumed as he was by sickly jealousy, regarding every man as a possible rival. Why did the schoolmaster regret that his wife had not accompanied him? Had she not twice called at the school recently under the pretext of explaining to the master why Achille and Philippe had been absent on sundry occasions? For some time past he, Savin, had compelled her to confess regularly once a week to Father Théodose, the Superior of the Capuchins, for it had occurred to him that the shame of avowal might stay her in her course along the road to infidelity. On her side, if in earlier times she had followed the Church observances merely in order to secure peace at home—for she was quite destitute of faith—she now repaired with some alacrity to the tribunal of penitence, for, like the other young devotees who dreamt of Father Théodose, she had rid herself of earlier prejudices, and begun to regard him as a superb and most delightful man.

'As it happens,' said Marc, with some little maliciousness, in response to Savin's declaration, 'I had the pleasure of meeting Madame Savin last Thursday. She was leaving the chapel on the Place des Capucins, and we had a brief chat. As all her words to me were most gracious, I thought I might express my regret at not seeing her with you to-day.'

The husband made a doleful gesture. His everlasting suspicions had reached such a point that he himself now went to Beaumont to deliver the bead work which he allowed his wife to do in secret in order to add a few indispensable coppers to his meagre salary. Their case was one of hidden wretchedness, with all the torments that make hells of the homes of needy employés, burdened with children, the embittered husband becoming an unbearable despot, and the gentle and pretty wife resigning herself in silence until she at last discovers some consolation.

'My wife neither has nor ought to have any opinion but mine,' Savin ended by declaring. 'It is in her name as well as my own, and in the names of many other parents—I repeat it—that I have made this application to you.... It is now for you to decide if you will act upon it. You will think the matter over.'

'I have thought it over, Monsieur Savin,' replied Marc, who had become grave again. 'Before removing that crucifix I understood fully what I was going to do; and since it is no longer there, I shall certainly not put it up again.'

On the following day a report spread through Maillebois that a deputation of parents, fathers and mothers, had called upon the schoolmaster, and that there had been a stormy explanation, a frightful scandal. But Marc soon understood whence the attack had really come, for chance acquainted him with the circumstances which had led to Savin's visit. Though pretty Madame Savin took no real interest in the affair, absorbed as she was in her desire for a little more personal happiness, she had none the less served as an instrument in the hands of Father Théodose;

for it was on being approached by her, on the Capuchin's behalf, that her husband had repaired to a secret interview with the latter, which interview had prompted him to call on Marc and endeavour to check a state of things which was so prejudicial to family morality and good order. No crucifixes in the schools indeed! Would that not mean indiscipline among the boys, and shamelessness among the girls and their mothers also? So the lean and little Savin, the Republican and anti-clerical, unhinged by his wretched spoilt life and his idiotic jealousy, had set forth to champion the cause of virtue, like an authoritarian, a topsy-turvy Catholic, who pictured the human paradise as a gaol, in which everything human ought to be subdued and crushed.

Besides, behind Father Théodose, Marc readily divined Brother Fulgence and his assistants, Brothers Gorgias and Isidore, who hated the secular school more than ever since it had been taking pupils from them. And behind the Brothers came Fathers Philibin and Crabot of the College of Valmarie, those powerful personages whose skilful unseen hands had been directing the whole campaign ever since the monstrous Simon affair. The accomplices in that slumbering crime seemed determined to defend it by other deeds of iniquity. At the outset Marc had guessed where the whole band, from the lowest to the highest, was crouching. But how could one seize and convict them? If Father Crabot, amiable and worldly, still showed himself constantly among the fine society of Beaumont, busily directing the steps of his penitents and ensuring the rapid fortune of his former pupils, his assistant, Father Philibin, had virtually disappeared, restricting himself entirely, so it seemed, to his absorbing duties as manager at Valmarie. Nothing transpired of the stealthy work which was so ardently pursued in the darkness, every moment being employed to ensure the triumph of the good cause. All that Marc himself could detect was the espionage attending his own movements. He was tracked with priestly caution, black figures were constantly prowling around him. None of his visits to the Lehmanns, none of his conversations with David could have remained unknown. And, as Salvan had said, the others tracked him because he was an impassioned soldier of truth and justice, because he was a witness who already possessed certain proofs, and whose avenging cry must be thrust back into his throat, even by extermination if necessary. To that task the frock and cassock wearers devoted themselves with increasing audacity, joined even by poor Abbé Quandieu, who felt grieved at having to place religion at the service of such iniquitous work, but who resigned himself to it in obedience to the behests of his Bishop, the mournful Monseigneur Bergerot, whom he visited every week at Beaumont to take his orders and console him in his defeat. Bishop and priest cast the cloak of their ministry over the sore devouring the Church whose respectful sons they were, hiding meantime their tears and their fears, unwilling to acknowledge the mortal danger into which they saw religion sinking.

One evening Mignot, on coming into the school from the playground, said to Marc in a fury:

'It's getting quite disgusting, monsieur! I've again caught Mademoiselle Rouzaire spying on us from the top of a ladder!'

Indeed, whenever the schoolmistress fancied that she would not be detected, she set a ladder against the wall dividing the two playgrounds, in order that she might ascertain what was going on in the boys' school. And Mignot accused her of sending secret reports on the subject to Mauraisin every week.

'Oh! let her pry,' Marc answered gaily. 'But there is no occasion for her to tire herself by climbing a ladder. I'll set the door wide open for her, if she desires it.'

'Ah! no, not that!' cried the assistant. 'Let her keep her place! If she tries it on again, I shall go round and pull her down by the legs!'

Marc, to his great satisfaction, was now gradually completing the conquest of Mignot. The latter, like a peasant's son whose one desire was to escape the plough, a man of average mind and character, who like so many others thought solely of his immediate interests, had always shown himself distrustful with Simon. Indeed, nothing good could come from a Jew, and so he had deemed it prudent to keep aloof from him. At the time of the trial, therefore, though he was sufficiently honest to refrain from overwhelming the innocent prisoner, he had not given the good and truthful evidence which might have saved him. At a later stage he had likewise placed himself on the defensive with Marc, with whom he thought it would be foolish to ally himself if he desired advancement. For nearly a whole year, therefore, he had displayed hostility, taking his meals at an eating-house, grudging the help he gave in the school work, and freely blaming his principal's attitude. At that time indeed he had been very thick with Mademoiselle Rouzaire, and willing, it seemed, to place himself at the orders of the Congregations. But Marc, instead of evincing any perturbation, had treated his assistant with unremitting kindness, as if he were desirous of giving him all necessary time to reflect and understand that his real interest lay on the side of truth and equity.

Indeed, in Marc's opinion, that big, calm young fellow, whose only passion was angling, offered an interesting subject for experiment. Though he became cowardly when he thought of the future, and was somewhat spoilt by the environment of ferocious egotism in which he found himself, there was nothing absolutely evil in his nature. In fact, he might be made an excellent school teacher and even a man of most upright mind if he were helped, sustained by one of energy and intelligence. The idea of experimenting in that sense attracted Marc, who felt well pleased as, little by little, he gained the confidence and affection of this wanderer, thereby proving the truth of the axiom in which he set all his hopes of future deliverance—that there is no man, even one on the road to perdition, who may not be made an artisan of progress. Mignot had been won over by the active gaiety, the beneficent glow of truth and justice which Marc set around him. He now took his meals with his principal, and had become, as it were, a member of the family.

'It is wrong of you not to distrust Mademoiselle Rouzaire,' he resumed. 'You have no idea, monsieur, of what she is capable. She would betray you a dozen times over in order to obtain good reports from her friend Mauraisin.'

Then, being in a confidential mood, he related how she had repeatedly urged him to listen at keyholes and report to her. He knew her well; she was a terrible woman, harsh and avaricious, despite all her varnish of exaggerated courtesy; and though she was big and bony, with a flat, freckled face, quite destitute of any charm, she ended by seducing everybody. As she herself boasted, she knew how to act. To the anti-clericals who angrily reproached her for taking her girls so often to church, she replied that she was compelled to comply with the desires of the parents under penalty of losing her pupils. To the clericals she gave the most substantial pledges, convinced as she was that they were the stronger party and that on their influence depended the best appointments even in the secular school world. In reality she was guided solely by her own interests, as she understood them, having inherited the instincts of a petty trader from her parents, who had kept a fruiterer's shop at Beaumont. She had not married, because she preferred to live as she listed, and, although she did not carry on with the priests, as was maliciously rumoured by evil tongues, it seemed certain that she had a soft spot in her heart for handsome Mauraisin, who, like the little man he was, admired women built after the fashion of gendarmes. Again, it was not true that she got drunk, though she was very fond of sweet liqueurs. If she occasionally looked very red when afternoon lessons began, it was simply because she ate abundantly and her digestive organs were out of order.

Marc made an indulgent gesture. 'She does not keep her school badly,' said he; 'the only thing that grieves me is the spirit of narrow pietism which she introduces into all her teaching. My boys and her girls are separated by an abyss, not merely by a wall. And when they meet one another, later, and think of marrying, they will belong to different worlds. But is not that the traditional custom? The warfare of the sexes largely arises from it.'

The young man did not mention the chief cause of his rancour against Mademoiselle Rouzaire, the reason which had impelled him to keep aloof from her. This was her abominable conduct in Simon's case. He remembered the quiet effrontery with which she had played the game of the Congregations at the trial at Beaumont, how she had heaped impudent falsehoods on the innocent prisoner, how she had accused him of giving immoral and anti-patriotic lessons to his pupils. And so Marc's intercourse with her since his appointment to Maillebois had never gone beyond the limits of strict politeness, such as the proximity of their homes required. She, however, having seen the young man strengthen his position, in such wise that his sudden downfall could now hardly be anticipated, had made attempts at reconciliation; for, in her anxiety to be always on the stronger side, she was not the woman to turn her back on the victorious. She had manœuvred particularly with the object of ingratiating herself with Geneviève, but the latter in this matter had hitherto shared Marc's opinions and kept her at a distance.

'At all events, monsieur,' Mignot concluded, 'I advise you to keep your eyes open. If I had listened to La Rouzaire I should have betrayed you a score of times. She never ceased questioning me about you, repeating to me that I was a stupid and would never succeed in getting into a decent position.... But you showed me great kindness, and you don't know what horrid things you saved me from; for one soon listens to those creatures when they promise you every kind of success. And, as I am on this subject, I hope you will excuse me if I venture to give you some advice. You ought to warn Madame Froment.'

'Warn her? What do you mean?'

'Yes, yes, I don't keep my eyes in my pockets. For some time past I have seen La Rouzaire prowling around your wife. It is "dear madame" here, a smile or a caress there, all kinds of advances, which would make me tremble if I were in your shoes.'

Marc, who felt greatly astonished, made a pretence of smiling: 'Oh! my wife has nothing to fear, she is warned,' said he. 'It is difficult for her to behave impolitely with a neighbour, particularly when one is connected by similar duties.'

Mignot did not insist, but he shook his head doubtfully, for his intercourse with the Froments had acquainted him with the secret drama which was slowly gathering in their home. However, it seemed as if he were unwilling to say all he knew. And Marc, on his side also, became silent, again mastered by the covert dread, the unacknowledged weakness which assailed and paralysed him whenever the possibility of a struggle between Geneviève and himself presented itself to his mind.

All at once the attack of the Congregations, which he had been anticipating ever since his visit to Salvan, took place. The campaign began with a virulent report from Mauraisin on the subject of the removal of the crucifix, and the scandal caused among the boys' parents by that act of religious intolerance. Savin's protest was duly recorded, and the Doloir and Bongard families were cited among those who blamed the proceeding. The incident was one of exceptional gravity, according to the Inspector, for it had occurred in a clerical-minded town, reputed for its frequent and numerously attended pilgrimages—a town indeed where it was necessary for the secular school to make concessions if it was to escape defeat from its Congregational rival. Mauraisin concluded, therefore, in favour of the removal of the schoolmaster, a sectarian of the worst kind, who had thus incautiously compromised the university cause. And his indictment was completed by the recital of a number of little facts, the harvest of all the daily espionage carried on by Mademoiselle Rouzaire, whose docile little girls, ever at Mass or at the Catechism classes, were contrasted with the idle, rebellious, unbelieving lads trained by that anarchist master, Froment.

Three days later Marc learnt that Count Hector de Sanglebœuf, the Catholic deputy, accompanied by two of his colleagues, had made an application on the subject to Prefect Hennebise. Sanglebœuf was evidently acquainted with Mauraisin's report, even if he had not helped to draft it in conjunction with his friend Father Crabot, who so frequently visited La Désirade; and the idea undoubtedly was to take that report as a basis in demanding the dismissal of Marc.

Hennebise, whose policy was to live at peace with everybody, and who constantly urged his subordinates to refrain from stirring up trouble, must have felt very worried by the incident, which might lead to disastrous complications. The Prefect's feelings were with Sanglebœuf, but it was dangerous to adhere publicly to the reactionary cause; so, while sympathising with the fiery anti Semite deputy, he explained that he was not master of the situation, for the law was precise and prevented him from removing a schoolmaster unless that step were proposed to him by Academy Inspector Le Barazer. With some relief, therefore, the Prefect referred the gentlemen to the Inspector, to whose office, which was also in the Préfecture buildings, they immediately repaired.

Le Barazer, an ex-professor who had become a prudent diplomatist, listened to them with a great show of attentive deference. He was a man of fifty, with a broad full-coloured face, and as yet scarcely a grey hair. He had grown up hating the Empire, and as he regarded secular education as one of the foundation stones of the Republic, he pursued by all available means the task of crushing the Congregational schools, whose triumph in his estimation would have killed France. But experience had shown him the danger of violent action, and he adhered to a long meditated and prudent course, which led some extremists to regard him as a very lukewarm Republican. Yet he was associated with some extraordinary victories achieved by long years of discreet and patient action. At Sangleboeuf's first words he made a show of disapproving Marc's removal of the crucifix, which, said he, was a useless demonstration, though he pointed out that nothing in the laws compelled the schoolmasters to allow religious emblems in the schools. It was all a mere question of usage, and he discreetly allowed it to be seen that this usage scarcely had his approval. Then, as Sangleboeuf, losing his temper, proclaimed himself a defender of the Church, and described the schoolmaster of Maillebois as a shameless individual who had stirred up the entire population against him, the Inspector placidly promised that he would study the question with all the care it deserved.

But Sangleboeuf wished to know if he had not received a report from his subordinate, Mauraisin; and whether that report did not suffice to show the gravity of the evil, the demoralisation, which could only be arrested by the immediate removal of the schoolmaster. At this question Le Barazer feigned great surprise. What report? Ah! yes, the quarterly report from the Elementary Inspector! Were its contents known, then? In any case, those reports were purely administrative, and merely supplied certain elements of appreciation for the Academy Inspector, whose duty it was to make personal inquiries. And thereupon Le Barazer dismissed the gentlemen, after again promising to take their application into full account.

A month went by, and nothing reached Marc, who daily expected a summons to the Préfecture. Le Barazer was doubtless following his usual tactics in order to gain time and exhaust the determination of the other side. Even as his friend Salvan had foretold, he was covertly supporting the young schoolmaster. But it was essential that the affair should not be aggravated, that increasing scandal should not compel his intervention; for assuredly he would not defend Marc beyond certain limits, but would end by sacrificing him if he thought that course expedient in order that the rest of his slow and opportunist campaign against the Congregational schools might not be interfered with. Unfortunately, things went from bad to worse at Maillebois. *Le Petit Beaumontais*, yielding to an inspiration which could be easily identified, started a vile campaign against Marc. As usual, it began with brief and vague paragraphs: Abominations were taking place in a neighbouring little town, and if necessary precise information would be given. Then schoolmaster Froment was plainly named, and under the headline 'The Scandal of Maillebois,' which was repeated almost daily, the paper published an extraordinary collection of tittle-tattle, the results of a pretended inquiry among the pupils and their parents, in which the schoolmaster was accused of the blackest crimes.

People were quite upset by these so-called revelations; the good Brothers and the Capuchins helped to spread terror abroad, and devotees never passed the Communal school without crossing themselves. Marc became conscious that he was in great peril; and Mignot bravely began to pack up his belongings, feeling certain that he would be swept away with his principal, whose side he had taken. Meantime Mademoiselle Rouzaire affected the most victorious airs when she conducted her girls to Mass; Father Théodose in his chapel, and even Curé Quandieu in his pulpit at St. Martin's, foretold the approaching restoration of God among the infidels, by which they meant that the crucifix would be soon set up again, with all solemnity, in the secular school; and, as a last blow, Marc, on meeting Darras, found him very cold, resolved to abandon him, for fear of losing the support of the minority of the Municipal Council.

'What can you expect, my dear fellow,' said the ex-Mayor; 'you have gone too far; we cannot follow you, at present at all events.... That blackbeetle Philis is watching me, and I should merely share your fate, which would be useless.'

In his despair Marc hastened to Salvan, whom he regarded as the only faithful supporter remaining to him. And he found him thoughtful, gloomy, almost embarrassed.

'Things are going badly,' said he. 'Le Barazer remains silent, seemingly anxious, and such a furious campaign is being waged around him that I fear he may abandon you.... Perhaps you acted too hastily.'

Marc's heart was wrung by a pang of grief, for he interpreted those last words as signifying that even Salvan abandoned him. 'You, you as well, my master!' he exclaimed.

But Salvan, full of emotion, caught hold of his hands. 'No, no, my lad, you must not doubt me; I remain on your side with all my heart. Only you can have no idea of the difficulties in which all of us have been placed by your action, simple and logical though it was. This Training College is suspected, denounced as a hot-bed of irreligion. Depinvilliers profits by it to exalt the services which the chaplain of his Lycée renders to the cause of national pacification, the reconcilement of all parties in the bosom of the Church. Even our Rector, the peaceable Forbes, is full of concern, fearing lest his tranquillity should be destroyed. Le Barazer, no doubt, is skilful, but does he possess the necessary strength of resistance?'

'What is to be done, then?'

'Nothing: one must wait. I can only repeat to you that you must show yourself prudent and courageous. For the rest we must rely on the force of truth and justice.'

During the next two months Marc displayed much brave serenity amid the outrages by which he was assailed each day. As if ignorant of the muddy tide beating against his door, he pursued his duties with wondrous gaiety and uprightness. Never had he accomplished more important or more useful work, devoting himself to his pupils, and teaching them, as much by example as by words, how necessary it was to continue working and to retain one's love for truth and justice amid the very worst events. To the filth, the bitter insults flung at him by his fellow townsmen, he replied with gentleness, kindliness, and sacrifice. He strove to make the children better than their fathers, he sowed the happy future in the furrows of the hateful present, he redeemed the crime of others at the cost of his own happiness. It was the thought of the young ones around him, the duty of helping to save them a little more each day from error and falsehood, that lent him so much calmness and enabled him to await the blow he expected with a quiet smile, like one who, every evening, felt well satisfied with the work accomplished during the day.

At last, one morning, *Le Petit Beaumontais* announced that the revocation of 'the ignoble poisoner of Maillebois' was signed. On the previous day Marc had heard of a fresh visit which the Count de Sanglebœuf had paid to the Préfecture, and he ceased to hope; his ruin was about to be consummated. The evening proved a very trying one. Whenever he quitted his classroom, and his boys, with their smiling faces and their fair and their dark little pates, were no longer near to remind him of the good time coming, he sank into sadness, and only after a struggle recovered the courage which he needed for the morrow. And so that particular evening proved particularly bitter. He thought of his work, destined to be so brutally interrupted—of those dearly-loved boys, whom he had taught perhaps for the last time, and whom he would not be allowed to save. They would be taken from him, handed over to some deformer of intellect and character, and it was the wreck of his ministry that made his heart bleed. He went to bed in such a gloomy mood that Geneviève gently, silently, cast her arms about him, as she still did occasionally from an impulse of wifely affection.

'You are worried, are you not, my poor darling?' she whispered.

He did not answer immediately. He knew that she shared his views less than ever, and he always avoided painful explanations in spite of his secret remorse at allowing her to drift away from him without attempting an effort to make her wholly his own. Indeed, if he himself had again ceased to call on her mother and grandmother, he lacked the courage to forbid her visits to that icy little house, though he well divined that their happiness was greatly endangered there. Each time that Geneviève returned from the Place des Capucins he felt that she belonged to him a little less than before. Recently, while the whole clerical pack was barking at his heels, he had learnt that the ladies had denied him on every side, blushing for their connection as if it were some unmerited shame that soiled their family.

'Why don't you answer me, dear?' Geneviève began again. 'Don't you think that I share your sorrow?'

He felt touched, and, returning her embrace, replied: 'Yes, I am grieved. But it is about matters in which you do not feel as I do, and, as I don't wish to reproach you, what is the use of confiding them to you? Still I may say I fear that in a few days we shall be here no longer.'

'How is that?'

'Oh! I shall certainly be sent elsewhere if I am not dismissed altogether. It is all over ... and we shall have to go away, I know not whither.'

She raised a cry of delight: 'Oh, my dear! so much the better! That is the best thing that can happen to us.'

He felt astonished, for her meaning at first escaped him. And when he questioned her she seemed somewhat embarrassed, and endeavoured to recall her words: 'Oh, I say that because, of course, it would be all the same to me if I did have to go away with you and our Louise. One may be happy anywhere.' But when he pressed her she added: 'Besides, if we went elsewhere we should no longer be worried by all the horrid things which go on here, and which might end by making us quarrel. I should be so happy if we could be alone in some little nook where nobody would come between us, where nothing from outside would try to separate us. Oh! let us go away to-morrow, dear!'

Several times already, in moments of affectionate self-abandonment, Marc had noticed in his wife that same dread of rupture, that desire, that need to remain wholly his. It was as if she said to him: 'Keep me on your heart, carry me away, so that none may tear me from your arms. I feel that I am being parted from you a little more each day, I shiver with the great chill which comes over me when I am no longer in your embrace.' And, with his dread of the inevitable, nothing could have upset him more.

'Go away, my love?' he answered; 'it is not enough to go away. But what joy you give me, and how grateful I feel to you for comforting me like that!'

Several more days elapsed and still the terrible letter expected from the Préfecture did not arrive. No doubt this was due to the fact that a fresh incident began to impassion the district and divert public attention from the secular school of Maillebois. For some time past Abbé Cognasse of Jonville, whose triumph was complete, had been meditating a great stroke, striving to induce Mayor Martineau to allow the parish to be consecrated to the Sacred Heart of Jesus. In all likelihood the idea had not come from the Abbé himself for every Thursday morning during the previous month he had been seen going to the College of Valmarie, where he had long conferences with Father Crabot. And a remark made by Férou, the schoolmaster at Le Moreux, was circulating, filling some folk with indignation and amusing others.

'If those dirty Jesuits bring their bullock's heart here, I will spit in their faces,' he had said.

Henceforth the worship of the Sacred Heart was absorbing the whole Christian faith, developing into a new Incarnation, a new Catholicism. The sickly vision of a poor creature stricken with hysteria—the sad and ardent Marie Alacoque—that real, gory heart half wrenched from an open bosom, was becoming the symbol of a baser faith, degraded, lowered to supply a need of carnal satisfaction. The ancient and pure worship of an immaterial Jesus, who had risen on high to join the Father, seemed to have become too delicate for modern souls lusting for terrestrial enjoyment; and it had been resolved to serve the very flesh of Jesus, His heart of flesh, to devotees, by way of daily sustenance, such as superstition and brutishness required. It was like a premeditated onslaught on human reason, an intentional degradation of the religion of former times in order that the mass of believers, bowed beneath the weight of falsehood, might become yet more stupefied and more servile. With the religion of the Sacred Heart only tribes of idolaters were left, fetichists who adored offal from a slaughter-house, and carried it, banner-wise, on a pike-head. And all the genius of the Jesuits was found therein—the humanisation of religion, God coming to man since centuries of effort had failed to lead man to God. It was necessary to give the ignorant multitude the only deity it understood, one made in its own image, gory and dolorous like itself, an idol of violent hues, whose brutish materiality would complete the transformation of the faithful into a herd of fat beasts, fit for slaughter. All conquests effected on reason are conquests effected on liberty, and it had become necessary to reduce France to that savage worship of the Sacred Heart, fit for the aborigines of some undiscovered continent, in order to hold it in submission beneath the imbecility of the Church's dogmas.

The first attempts had been made on the very morrow of the great defeats, amid the grief arising from the loss of the two provinces. Then already the Church had availed herself of the public confusion to endeavour to consecrate France to the Sacred Heart—France, which after being chastised so heavily by the hand of God, repented of her sins. And at last, on the highest summit of that great revolutionary city of Paris, the Church had reared that Sacred Heart, palpitating and gory red like the hearts which one sees hanging from hooks in butchers' shops. From that summit it bled over the entire land, to the farthest depths of the country districts. And if at Montmartre it kindled the adoration of the gentility, of ladies and gentlemen belonging to the administrative services, the magistracy and the army, with what emotion must it not infect the simple, the ignorant, and the devout of the villages and hamlets! It became the national emblem of repentance, of the country's self-relinquishment in the hands of the Church. It was embroidered in the centre of the tricolor flag, whose three colours became mere symbols of the azure of heaven, the lilies of the Virgin, and the blood of the martyrs. And huge, swollen, and streaming with gore, it hung thus like the new Deity of degenerate Catholicism, offered to the base superstition of enslaved France.

At first it had been Father Crabot's idea to triumph at Maillebois, the chief place in the canton, by consecrating that little town to the Sacred Heart. But he had become anxious, for at Maillebois there was a manufacturing suburb inhabited by some hundreds of working men who were beginning to send Socialist representatives to the Municipal Council. Thus, in spite of the Brothers and the Capuchins, he had feared some sensational repulse. All considered, it was better to act at Jonville, where the ground appeared well prepared. If successful there, one might always repeat the experiment on a larger stage, some other time.

Abbé Cognasse now reigned at Jonville, which schoolmaster Jauffre had gradually handed over to him. Jauffre's guiding principle was a very simple one. As Clericalism was sweeping through the region, why should he not allow it to waft him to the headmastership of some important school at Beaumont? Thus, after prompting his wife to make advances to the parish priest, he himself had openly gone over to the Church, ringing the bell, chanting at the offices, taking his pupils to Mass every Sunday. Mayor Martineau, who, following Marc, had been an anti-clerical in former times, was at first upset by the new schoolmaster's doings. But what could he say to a man who was so well off and who explained so plausibly that it was wrong to be against the priests? Thus Martineau was shaken in his ideas and allowed the other to follow his course, till, at last, prompted thereto by the beautiful Madame Martineau, he himself declared to the parish council that it was best to live in agreement with the curé. After that, a year sufficed for Abbé Cognasse to become the absolute master of the parish, his influence no longer being counterbalanced by that of the schoolmaster, who, indeed, willingly walked behind him, confident that he would derive a handsome profit from his submissiveness.

Nevertheless, when the idea of consecrating Jonville to the Sacred Heart was propounded, some dismay and resistance arose. Nobody knew whence that idea had come, nobody could have said by whom it had been first mooted. However, Abbé Cognasse, with his eager militant nature, immediately made it his business in the hope of gaining great personal glory should he be the first priest of the region to win an entire parish over to God. He made such a stir, indeed, that Monseigneur Bergerot, in despair at the threat of a new superstition, and grieved by its base idolatry, summoned him to Beaumont, where, however, after a scene which proved, it was rumoured, both terrible and pathetic, the Bishop once again was compelled to give way. But, on two occasions, the parish council of Jonville held tumultuous meetings, several members angrily desiring to know what profit they would all derive from the consecration of the parish to the Sacred Heart. For a moment it seemed as if the affair were condemned and buried. But Jauffre also made a trip to Beaumont, and, though nobody guessed exactly what personage he saw there, he no sooner came back than, in a gentle, insidious manner, he resumed the negotiations with the parish council.

The question was what the parish would gain by consecrating itself to the Sacred Heart. Well, first of all, several ladies of Beaumont promised presents to the church, a silver chalice, an altar cloth, some flower vases, and a big statue of the Saviour, with a huge, flaming, bleeding heart painted on it. Then, too, said Jauffre, there was talk of giving a dowry of five hundred francs to the most deserving Maiden of the Virgin when she married. But the council seemed to be most impressed by the promise of setting up a branch establishment of the Order of the Good Shepherd, where two hundred girls would work at fine linen, chemises, petticoats, and knickers, for some of the great Parisian shops. The peasants at once pictured all their daughters working for the good Sisters, and speculated on the large amount of money which such an establishment would probably bring into the district.

At last it was decided that the ceremony should take place on June 10 (a Sunday), and, as Abbé Cognasse pointed out, never was festival favoured by brighter sunshine. For three days his servant, the terrible Palmyre, with the help of Madame Jauffre and the beautiful Madame Martineau, had been decorating the church with evergreens and hangings, lent by the inhabitants. The ladies of Beaumont, Présidente Gragnon, Générale Jarousse, Préfete Hennebise—and even, so it was said, Madame Lemarrois, the wife of the radical mayor and deputy,—had presented the parish with a superb tricolor flag on which the Sacred Heart was embroidered, with the motto: 'God and Country.' And Jauffre himself was to carry that flag, walking on the right hand of the Mayor of Jonville. An extraordinary concourse of important personages arrived during the morning: many notabilities of Beaumont, with the ladies who had presented the flag; Philis, the Mayor of Maillebois, with the clerical majority of his council, as well as a shoal of cassocks and frocks; a grand-vicar, delegated by Monseigneur the Bishop, Father Théodose and other Capuchins, Brother Fulgence and his assistant Brothers, Father Philibin and even Father Crabot, both of whom were surrounded and saluted with the greatest deference. But people noticed the absence of Abbé Quandieu, who, according to his own account, had been laid up by a violent attack of gout at the last moment.

At three o'clock in the afternoon a band of music, which had come from the chief town, struck up an heroic march on the Place de l'Église. Then appeared the parish councillors, all wearing their scarves, and headed by Mayor Martineau and schoolmaster Jauffre, the latter of whom grasped the staff of his flag with both hands. A halt ensued until the band had finished playing. A dense crowd of peasant families in their Sunday best, and ladies in full dress, had gathered round, waiting. Then, all at once, the principal door of the church was thrown wide open, and Curé Cognasse appeared in rich sacerdotal vestments, followed by numerous members of the clergy, the many priests who had hastened to Jonville from surrounding spots. Chants arose, and all the people prostrated themselves devoutly during the solemn blessing of the flag. The pathetic moment came when Mayor Martineau and the members of the council knelt beneath the folds of the symbolic standard, which Jauffre held slantwise above them in order that one might the better see the gory heart embroidered amid the three colours. And then in a loud voice the Mayor read the deed officially consecrating the parish of Jonville to that heart.

Women wept and men applauded. A gust of blissful insanity arose into the clear sunlight, above the blare of the brass instruments and the beating of the drums which had again struck up a triumphal march. And the procession entered the church, the clergy, the Mayor, and the council, still and ever attended by the schoolmaster and the flag. Then came the benediction of the Holy Sacrament; the monstrance glittering like a great star on the altar, amid all the lighted candles, while the municipality again knelt down most devoutly. And afterwards Abbé Cognasse began to speak with fiery eloquence, exulting at the sight of the representatives of civil authority sheltering themselves beneath the banner of the Sacred Heart, prostrating themselves before the Holy Sacrament, abdicating all pride and rebellion in the hands of the Deity, relying on Him alone to govern and save France. Did not this signify the end of impiety, the Church mistress of men's souls and bodies, sole representative of power and authority on earth? Ah! she would not long delay to restore happiness to her well-beloved eldest Daughter, who at last repented of her errors, submitted, and sought nothing but salvation. Every parish would end by following the example of Jonville, the whole country would give itself to the Sacred Heart, France would recover her empire over the world by the worship of the national flag now transformed into the flag of Jesus! Cries of ecstatic intoxication burst forth, and the splendid ceremony came to an end in the sacristy, whither the council, headed by the Mayor, repaired to sign the deed on parchment which set forth that the whole parish of Jonville had for ever consecrated itself to the Divine Heart, the civil power piously renouncing its claims in favour of the religious power.

But when the party quitted the church a scandalous scene occurred. Among the crowd was Férou, the schoolmaster at Le Moreux, clad in a wretched, tattered frock coat and looking more emaciated, more ardent than ever. He had sunk to the worst tortures of indebtedness, he was pursued for francs and half francs which he had borrowed, for he could no longer obtain on credit the six pounds of bread which he needed daily to feed his exhausted wife and his three lean and ailing daughters. Even before it was due, his paltry salary of a hundred francs a month disappeared in that ever-widening gulf, and the little sum which he received as parish clerk was constantly being attached by creditors. His growing and incurable misery had increased the contempt of the peasants who were all at their ease, and who looked askance at knowledge as it did not even feed the master appointed to teach it. And Férou, the only man of intelligence and culture in that abode of dense ignorance, grew more and more exasperated at the thought that he, the man who knew, should be the poor one, whereas the ignorant were rich. Feverish rebellion against such social iniquity came upon him, he was maddened by the sufferings of those who were dear to him, and dreamt of destroying this abominable world by violence.

As he stood there he caught sight of Saleur, the Mayor of Le Moreux, who, wishing to make himself agreeable to the triumphant Abbé Cognasse, had come over to Jonville, arrayed in a fine new frock coat. Peace now reigned between his parish and the priest, though the latter still grumbled at having to walk several miles to say Mass for people who might very well have kept a priest of their own. However, all the esteem which had departed from the thin, ghastly, ill-paid, penniless, and deeply indebted schoolmaster had now gone to the sturdy and flourishing priest who was so much better off, and who turned every baptism, wedding, and burial into so much money. Beaten, as was only natural, in that unequal duel, Férou was no longer able to control his rage.

'Well, Monsieur Saleur,' he exclaimed, 'here's a carnival and no mistake! Aren't you ashamed to lend yourself to such ignominy?'

Though Saleur was not at heart with the priests, this remark vexed him. He construed it as an attack upon his own *bourgeois* position as an enriched grazier, living on his income in a pretty house, repainted and decorated at his own expense. So he sought for dignified words of reprimand: 'You would do better to keep quiet, Monsieur Férou. The shame belongs to those who can't even succeed sufficiently to lead respectable lives.'

Irritated by this rejoinder, which smacked of the low standard of morality that brought him so much suffering, Férou was about to reply when his anger was diverted by the sight of Jauffre.

'Ah! colleague,' said he, 'so it's you who carry their banner of falsehood and imbecility! That's a fine action for an educator of the lowly and humble ones of our democracy! You know very well that the priest's gain is the schoolmaster's loss.'

Jauffre, like a man who had an income of his own, and who, moreover, was well pleased with what he had done, replied with compassionate yet crushing contempt: 'Before judging others, my poor comrade, you would do well to provide your daughters with shifts to hide their nakedness!'

At this Férou lost all self-control. With his unkempt hair bristling on his head, and a savage gleam in his wild eyes, he waved his long arms and cried: 'You gang of bigots! you pack of Jesuits! Carry your bullock's heart about, worship it, eat it raw, and become, if you can, even more bestial and imbecile than you are already!'

A crowd gathered around the blasphemer, hoots and threats arose, and things would have turned out badly for him if Saleur, like a prudent Mayor, alarmed for the good name of his commune, had not extricated him from the hostile throng and led him away by the arm.

On the morrow the incident was greatly exaggerated; on all sides people talked of execrable sacrilege. Indeed, *Le Petit Beaumontais* related that the schoolmaster of Le Moreux had spat on the national flag of the Sacred Heart at the very moment when worthy Abbé Cognasse was blessing that divine emblem of repentant and rescued France. And in its ensuing number it announced that the revocation of schoolmaster Férou was a certainty. If that were so, the consequences would be serious, for as Férou had not completed his term of ten years' duty as a teacher he would have to perform some years' military service. And, again, while he was in barracks, what would become of his wife and daughters, those woeful creatures for whom he was already unable to provide? He gone, would they not utterly starve to death?

When Marc heard of what had happened he went to see Salvan at Beaumont. This time the newspaper's information was correct, the revocation of Férou was about to be signed, Le Barazer was resolved on it. And as Marc nevertheless begged his old friend to attempt some intervention, the other sadly refused to do so.

'No, no, it would be useless,' he said; 'I should simply encounter inflexible determination. Le Barazer cannot act otherwise; at least, such is his conviction. Opportunist as he is, he finds in that course a means of ridding himself of the other difficulties of the present time.... And you must not complain too much; for if his severity falls on Férou it is in order that he may spare you.'

At this Marc burst into protest, saying how much he was upset and grieved by such a *dénouement*.

'But you are not responsible, my dear fellow,' Salvan replied. 'He is casting that prey to the clericals because they require one, and because he thus hopes to save a good workman like yourself. It is a very *distinguée* solution, as somebody said to me yesterday.... Ah! how many tears and how much blood must necessarily flow for the slightest progress to be accomplished, how many poor corpses must fill up the ditches in order that the heroes may pass on!'

Salvan's forecast was fulfilled to the very letter. Two days afterwards Férou was dismissed, and, rather than resign himself to military service, he fled to Belgium, full of exasperation at the thought that justice should be denied him. He hoped to find some petty situation at Brussels, which would enable him to send for his wife and children, and make himself a new home abroad. He even ended by declaring that he felt relieved at having escaped from the university galleys, and that he now breathed freely, like a man who was at last at liberty to think and act as he listed.

Meantime his wife installed herself with her three little girls in two small, sordid rooms at Maillebois, where, with all bravery, she at once began to ply her needle as a seamstress, though she found herself unable to earn enough for daily bread. Marc visited her and helped her as far as he could, feeling quite heartbroken at the sight of her pitiable wretchedness. And a remorseful feeling clung to him, for the affair of the crucifix appeared to be forgotten amid the keen emotion roused by the sacrilege of Jonville and the revocation which had followed it. *Le Petit Beaumontais* triumphed noisily, and the Count de Sangleboeuf promenaded the town with victorious airs as if his friends, the Brothers, the Capuchins, and the Jesuits, had now become the absolute masters of the department. And then life followed its course, pending the time when the struggle would begin again, on another field.

One Sunday Marc was surprised to see his wife come home carrying a Mass-book. 'What! have you been to church?' he asked her.

'Yes,' she answered,' I have just taken the Communion.' He looked at her, turning pale the while, penetrated by a sudden chill, a quiver, which he strove to hide. 'You do that now, and you did not tell me of it?' said he.

On her side she feigned astonishment, though, according to her wont, she remained very calm and gentle: 'Tell you of it—why?' she asked. 'It is a matter of conscience. I leave you free to act according to your views, so I suppose I may act according to mine.'

'No doubt; all the same, for the sake of a good understanding between us, I should have liked to have known.'

'Well, you know now. I do not hide it, as you may see. But we shall, none the less, remain good friends, I hope.'

She added nothing more, and he lacked the strength to tell her of all that he felt seething within him, to provoke the explanation which he knew to be imperative. But the day remained heavy with silence. This time some connecting link had certainly snapped and sundered them.

CHAPTER III

Some months elapsed, and day by day Marc found himself confronted by the redoubtable question: Why had he married a woman whose belief was contrary to his own? Did not he and Geneviève belong to two hostile spheres, divided by an abyss, and would not their disagreement bring them the most frightful torture? Some scientists were suggesting that when people desired to marry they should undergo proper examination, and provide themselves with certificates setting forth that they were free from all physical flaws. The young man for his part felt convinced that all such certificates ought also to state that the holder's heart and mind were free from every form of inherited or acquired imbecility. Two beings, ignorant one of the other, coming from different worlds, as it were, with contradictory and hostile notions, could only torture and destroy each other. And yet how great an excuse was, at the outset, furnished by the imperious blindness of love, and how difficult it was to solve the question in some particular cases, which were often those instinct with most charm and tenderness!

Marc did not yet accuse Geneviève—he merely dreaded lest she should become a deadly weapon in the hands of those priests and monks against whom he was waging war. As the Church had failed to strike him down by intriguing with his superiors, it must now be thinking of dealing him a blow in the heart by destroying his domestic happiness. That was essentially the device of the Jesuits, the everlasting manœuvre of the father-confessor, who helps on the work of Catholic domination in stealthy fashion, like a worldly psychologist well acquainted with the passions and the means they offer for triumphing over the human beast, who, fondled and satiated, may then be strangled. To glide into a home, to set oneself between husband and wife, to capture the latter and thereby destroy the man whom the Church wishes to get rid of, no easier and more widely adopted stratagem than this is known to the black whisperers of the confessional.

The Church, having taken possession of woman, has used her as its most powerful weapon of propaganda and enthralment. At the first moment an obstacle certainly arose. Was not woman all shame and perdition, a creature of sin, and terror, before whom the very saints trembled? Vile nature had set its trap in her, she was the source of life, she was life itself, the contempt of which was taught by the Church. And so for a moment the latter denied a soul to woman, the creature from whom men of purity fled to the desert, in danger of succumbing if the evening breeze wafted to them merely the odour of her hair. Beauty and passion being cast out of the religious system, she became the mere embodiment of all that was condemned, all that was regarded as diabolical, denounced as the craft of Satan, all against which prayer, mortification, and strict and perpetual chastity were enjoined. And in the desire to crush sexuality in woman, the ideal woman was shown sexless, and a virgin was enthroned as queen of heaven.

But the Church ended by understanding the irresistible sexual power of woman over man, and in spite of its repugnance, in spite of its terror, decided to employ it as a means to conquer and enchain man. That great flock of women, weakened by an abasing system of education, terrorised by the fear of hell, degraded to the status of serfs by the hatred and harshness of priests, might serve as an army. And as man was ceasing to believe and turning aside from the altars, an effort to bring him back to them might be attempted with the help of woman's Satanic but ever victorious charm. She need only withhold herself from man, and he would follow her to the very foot of the shrines. In this, no doubt, there was much immoral inconsistency; but had not the Church lost much of its primitive sternness, and had not the Jesuits appeared upon the scene to fight the great fight on the new field of casuistry and accommodation with the world? From that time, then, the Church handled woman more gently and skilfully than before. It still refused to take her to wife, for it feared and loathed her as the embodiment of sin, but it employed her to ensure its triumph. Its policy was to keep her to itself, by stupefying her as formerly, by holding her in a state of perpetual mental infancy. That much ensured, it turned her into a weapon of war, confident that it would vanquish incredulous man by setting pious woman before him. And in woman the Church always had a witness at the family hearth, and was able to exert its influence even in the most intimate moments of conjugal life, whenever it desired to plunge resisting men into the worst despair. Thus, at bottom, woman still remained the human animal, and the priests merely made use of her in order to ensure the triumph of their creed.

Marc easily reconstituted the early phases of Geneviève's life: in childhood, the pleasant convent of the Sisters of the Visitation, with all sorts of devout attractions; the evening prayer on one's knees beside the little white bed; the providential protection promised to those who were obedient; the lovely stories of Christians saved from lions, of guardian angels watching over children, and carrying the pure souls of the well-beloved to heaven, such indeed as Monsieur le Curé related in the dazzling chapel. Afterwards came years of skilful preparation for the first Communion, with the extraordinary mysteries of the Catechism enshrouded in fearsome obscurity, for ever disturbing the reason, and kindling all the perverse fever of mystical curiosity. Then in the first troublous hour of maidenhood the young girl, enraptured with her white gown, her first bridal gown, was affianced to Jesus, united to the divine lover, whose gentle sway she accepted for ever; and man might come afterwards, he would find himself forestalled by an influence which would dispute his possession of her with all the haunting force of remembrance. Again and again throughout her life woman would see the candles sparkling, feel the incense filling her with languor, hark back to the wakening of her senses amid the mysterious whispering of the confessional and the languishing rapture of the Holy Table. She would spend her youth encompassed by the worst prejudices, nourished with the errors and falsehoods of ages, and, above all things, kept in close captivity in order that nothing of the real world might reach her. Thus the girl of sixteen or seventeen, on quitting the good Sisters of the Visitation, was a miracle of perversion and stultification, one whose natural vision had been dimmed, one who knew nothing of herself nor of others, and who in the part she would play in love and wifehood would bring, apart from her beauty, nought save religious poison, the evil ferment of every disorder and every suffering.

Marc pictured Geneviève, somewhat later, in the devout little house on the Place des Capucins. It was there that he had first seen her in the charge of her grandmother and mother, the chief care of whose vigilant affection had been to complete the convent work by setting on one side everything that might have made the girl a creature of truth and reason. It was enough that she should follow the Church's observances like an obedient worshipper; she was told that she need take no interest in other things; she was prepared for life by being kept quite blind to it. Some effort on Marc's part was already necessary to enable him to recall her such as she had been at the time of their first interviews—delightfully fair, with a refined and gentle face, so desirable too with the flush of her youth, the penetrating perfume of her blond beauty, that he only vaguely remembered whether she had then shown much intelligence and sense. A gust of passion had transported them both; he had felt that she shared his flame; for, however chilling might have been her education, she had inherited from her father a real craving for love.

In matters of intellect she was doubtless no fool; he must have deemed her similar to other young girls, of whom one knows nothing; and certainly he had resolved to look into all that after their marriage. But when he now recalled their first years at Jonville he perceived how slight had been his efforts to know her better and make her more wholly his own. They had spent those years in mutual rapture, in such passionate intoxication that they had remained unconscious even of their moral differences. She showed real intelligence in many things, and he had not cared to worry her about the singular gaps which he had occasionally discovered in her understanding. As she ceased to follow the observances of the Church he imagined that he had won her over to his views, though he had not even taken the trouble to instruct her in them. He now suspected that there must have been some little cowardice on his part, some dislike of the bother of re-educating her entirely, and also some fear of encountering obstacles, and spoiling the adorable quietude of their love. Indeed, as their life was all happiness, why should he have sought a cause of strife, particularly as he had felt convinced that their great love would suffice to ensure their good understanding whatever might arise?

But now the crisis was at hand, heavy with menace. When Salvan had interested himself in the marriage he had pointed out to Marc that if husband and wife were ill-assorted there was always some fear for the future; and to tranquillise his own conscience with respect to the young man's case it had been necessary that he should accept the view adopted by Marc, that when a young couple adored one another it was possible for the husband to make his wife such as he desired her to be. Indeed, when an ignorant young girl is handed over to a man whom she loves, is it not in his power to re-create her in his own image? He is her god, and may mould her afresh by the sovereign might of love. Such is the theory, but how often is it put into practice? Languor, blindness, come upon the man himself; and in Marc's case it was only long afterwards that he had realised how ignorant he had really remained of Geneviève's mind—a mind which, awaking according to the play of circumstances, revealed itself at last as that of an unknown, antagonistic woman.

The effects of the warm bath of religiosity in which Geneviève had grown up were still there. The adored woman, whom Marc had imagined to be wholly his own, was possessed by the indelible, indestructible past, in which he had no share whatever. He perceived with stupefaction that they had nothing in common, that though he had made her wife and mother, he had in no degree modified her brain, fashioned from her cradle days by skilful hands. Ah! how bitterly he now regretted that, in the first months of their married life, he had not striven to conquer the mind that existed behind the charming face which he had covered with his kisses! He ought not to have abandoned himself to his happiness, he ought to have striven to re-educate the big child who hung so amorously about his neck. As it had been his desire to make her entirely his own, why had he not shown himself a prudent, sensible man, whose reason remained undisturbed by the joys of love? If he suffered now it was by reason of his vain illusions, his idleness, and his egotism in refraining from action, from the fear of spoiling the felicity of his dalliance.

But the danger had now become so serious that he resolved to contend with it. A last excuse for avoiding anything like rough intervention remained to him: respect for another's freedom, tolerance of whatever might be the sincere faith of his life's companion. With amorous weakness he had consented to a religious marriage, and subsequently to the baptism of his daughter Louise, and, in the same way, he now lacked the strength to forbid his wife's attendance at Mass, Communion, and Confession, if her belief lay in such observances. Yet times had changed; he might have pleaded that at the date of his wedding, and again at the period of his daughter's birth, he had been quite indifferent to Church matters, whereas things were very different now that he had formally rejected the Church and its creed. He had imposed a duty on himself, he ought to set an example, he ought not to allow in his own home that which he condemned in the homes of others. If he, the secular schoolmaster, who showed such marked hostility to the interference of priests in the education of the young, should suffer his wife to go to Mass and take little Louise with her, would he not render himself liable to reproach? Nevertheless, he did not feel that he had the right to prevent those things, so great was his innate respect for liberty of conscience. Thus, confronted as he was by the imperious necessity of defending his happiness, he perceived no other available weapons, particularly in his own home, than discussion, persuasion, and the daily teaching of life in all that it has of a logical and healthful nature. That which he ought to have done at the outset, he must attempt now, not only in order to win his Geneviève over to healthy human truth, but also to prevent their dear Louise from following her into the deadly errors of Roman Catholicism.

For the moment, however, the case of Louise, now seven years of age, seemed less urgent. Moreover, though Marc was convinced that a child's first impressions are the keenest and the most tenacious, circumstances compelled a waiting policy with respect to his little girl. He had been obliged to let her attend the neighbouring school, where Mademoiselle Rouzaire was already filling her mind with Bible history. There were also prayers at the beginning and at the end of lessons, Sunday attendance at Mass, benedictions and processions. The schoolmistress had certainly bowed assent with a sharp smile when Marc had exacted from her a promise that his daughter should not be required to follow any religious exercises. But the girl was still so young that it seemed ridiculous to insist on preserving her from contamination in this fashion; besides which, Marc was not always at hand to make sure whether she said prayers with the other children or not. That which disgusted him with Mademoiselle Rouzaire was less the clerical zeal which seemed to consume her than her hypocrisy, the keen personal interest which guided all her actions. The woman's lack of real faith, her mere exploitation of religious sentimentality for her own advantage, was so apparent that even Geneviève, whose uprightness still remained entire, was wounded by it, and for this reason had repulsed the other's advances.

The schoolmistress, indeed, wishing to worm her way into Marc's home and scenting the possibility of a drama there, had suddenly manifested great friendship for her neighbour. What delight and glory it would be if she could render the Church a service in that direction, separate the wife from the husband, and strike the secular schoolmaster down at his own fireside! She therefore showed herself very amiable and insinuating, ever keeping on the watch behind the party-wall, hoping for some opportunity which would enable her to intervene and console the 'poor persecuted little wife.' At times she risked allusions, expressions of sympathy, words of advice: 'It was so sad when husband and wife were not of the same faith! And assuredly one must not wreck one's soul, so it was best to offer some gentle resistance.' On two occasions Mademoiselle Rouzaire had the pleasure of seeing Geneviève shed tears. But afterwards the young wife, feeling very uneasy, drew away from her, and avoided all further confidential chats. That mealy-mouthed woman, with her 'gendarme' build, her fondness for anisette, and her chatter about the priests,—'who, after all, were not different from other men, and of whom it was wrong to speak badly,'—inspired her with unconquerable repugnance. Thus repulsed, Mademoiselle Rouzaire felt her hatred for her neighbours increase, and visited her spite on little Louise by instructing her most carefully in religious matters, in spite of the paternal prohibition.

If Marc was not seriously concerned as yet about his daughter, he understood that it was urgent he should act in order to prevent his beloved Geneviève from being wrested from him. It was now plain to him that her religious views had revived at her grandmother's house. The pious little home on the Place des Capucins was like a hot-bed of mystical contagion, where a faith, which had not been extinguished, but which had died down amid the first joys of human love, was bound to be fanned into flame once more. Had they remained at Jonville in loving solitude, he, Marc, might have sufficed for Geneviève's yearning passion. But at Maillebois foreign elements had intervened between them. That terrible Simon case had brought about the first snap, and then had come its consequences, the struggle between himself and the Congregations, and the liberating mission which he had undertaken. Besides, they had no longer remained alone; a stream of people and things now flowed between them, growing ever wider and wider, and they could already foresee the day when they would be utter strangers, one to the other.

At present Geneviève met some of Marc's bitterest enemies at Madame Duparque's. The young man learnt at last that the terrible grandmother, after years of humble solicitation, had obtained the favour of being included among Father Crabot's penitents. The Rector of Valmarie usually reserved his services as confessor for the fine ladies of Beaumont, and only some very powerful reasons could have induced him to confess that old *bourgeoise*, who, socially, was of no account whatever. And not only did he receive her at the chapel of Valmarie, but he did her the honour to repair to the Place des Capucins whenever an attack of gout confined her to her armchair. He there met other personages of the cloth, Abbé Quandieu, Father Théodose, and Brother Fulgence, who became partial to that pious nook all shadows and silence, that well-closed little house where their conclaves, it seemed, might pass unperceived. Nevertheless, rumours circulated, some evil-minded people saying that the house was indeed the clerical faction's secret headquarters, the hidden laboratory, where its most important resolutions were prepared. Yet how could one seriously suspect the modest dwelling of two old ladies, who certainly had every right to receive their friends? The latter's shadows were scarcely seen; Pélagie, the servant, swiftly and softly closed the door upon them; not a face ever appeared at the windows, not a murmur filtered through the sleepy little façade. Everything was very dignified—great deference was shown for that highly respectable dwelling.

But Marc regretted that he had not gone there more frequently. Assuredly he had made a great mistake in abandoning Geneviève to the two old ladies, allowing her to spend whole days in their company with little Louise. His presence would have counteracted the contagion of that sphere; had he been there the others would have restrained the stealthy attacks which, as he well realised, they made upon his ideas and his person. Geneviève, as if conscious of the danger with which the peace of her home was threatened, occasionally offered some resistance, struggling to avoid hostilities with the husband whom she still loved. For instance, on returning to the observances of the Church, she had chosen Abbé Quandieu as her confessor instead of Father Théodose, whom Madame Duparque had sought to impose on her. The young woman was conscious of the warlike ardour that lurked behind the Capuchin's handsome face, his beautifully-kept black beard, and his glowing eyes, which filled his penitents with dreams of rapture; whereas the Abbé was a prudent and gentle man, a fatherly confessor, whose frequent silence was full of sadness—one, too, in whom she vaguely divined a friend, one who suffered from the fratricidal warfare of the times, and longed for peace among all workers of good will.

Geneviève, indeed, was yet at a stage of loving tenderness, when her mind, though gradually becoming clouded, still manifested some anxiety before it finally sank into mystical passion. But day by day she was confronted by more serious assaults, and yielded more and more to the disturbing influence of her relatives, whose unctuous gestures and caressing words slowly benumbed her. In vain did Marc now repair more frequently to the Place des Capucins; he could no longer arrest the poison's deadly work.

As yet, however, there was no attempt to enforce authority, no brutal roughness. Geneviève was merely enticed, flattered, cajoled, with gentle hands. And no violent words were spoken of her husband; on the contrary, he was said to be a man deserving of all pity, a sinner whose salvation was most desirable. The unhappy being! He knew not what incalculable harm he was doing to his country, how many children's souls he was wrecking, sending to hell, through his obstinate rebellion and pride! Then, at first vaguely, and afterwards more and more plainly, a desire was expressed in Geneviève's presence that she might devote herself to the most praiseworthy task of converting that sinner, redeeming that guilty man, whom, in her weakness, she still loved. What joy and glory would be hers if she should lead him back to religion, arrest his rageful work of destruction, save him, and thereby save his innocent victims from eternal damnation! For several months, with infinite craft, the young woman was in this wise worked upon, prepared for the enterprise expected of her, with the evident hope of bringing about conjugal rupture by fomenting a collision between the two irreconcilable principles which she and her husband represented—she a woman of the past, full of the errors of the ages—he a man of free thought, marching towards the future. And in time the much-sought, inevitable developments appeared.

The conjugal life of Marc and Geneviève grew sadder every day—that life so gay and loving once, when their kisses had perpetually mingled with their merry laughter. They had not yet reached the quarrelling stage; but, as soon as they found themselves alone together and unoccupied, they felt embarrassed. Something of which they never spoke seemed to be growing up between them, chilling them more and more, prompting them to enmity. On Marc's side there was a growing consciousness that she who was bound up with every hour of his life, she whom he embraced at night, was a woman foreign to him, one whose ideas and sentiments he reprobated. And on Geneviève's side there was a similar feeling, an exasperating conviction that she was regarded as an ignorant, unreasonable child, one who was still adored but with a love laden with much dolorous compassion. Thus their first wounds were imminent.

One night, when they were in bed, encompassed by the warm darkness, while Marc held Geneviève in a mute embrace as if she were some sulking child, she suddenly burst into bitter sobs, exclaiming: 'Ah! you love me no longer!'

'No longer love you, my darling!' he replied; 'why do you say that?'

'If you loved me you would not leave me in such dreadful sorrow! You turn away from me more and more each day. You treat me as if I were some ailing creature, sickly or insane. Nothing that I may say seems of any account to you. You shrug your shoulders at it. Ah! I feel it plainly, you are growing more and more impatient; I am becoming a worry, a burden to you.'

Though Marc's heart contracted, he did not interrupt her, for he wished to learn everything.

'Yes,' she resumed, 'unhappily for me I can see things quite plainly. You take more interest in the last of your boys than you do in me. When you are downstairs with the boys, in the classroom, you become impassioned, you pour out your whole soul, you exert yourself to explain the slightest things to them, and laugh and play with them like an elder brother. But directly you come upstairs you get gloomy again; you can think of nothing to say to me, you look ill at ease, like a man who's worried by his wife and tired of her.... Ah! God, God, how unhappy I am!'

Again she burst into sobs.

Then Marc, making up his mind, gently responded: 'I dared not tell you the cause of my sadness, darling, but if I suffer it is precisely because I find in you all that you reproach me with. You are never with me now. You spend whole days elsewhere, and when you come home you bring with you an air of unreason and death, which ravages our poor home. It is you who no longer speak to me. Your mind is always wandering, deep in some dim dream, even while you are sewing, or serving the meals, or attending to our little Louise. It is you who treat me with indulgent pity, as if I were a guilty man, perhaps one unconscious of his crime; and it is you who will soon have ceased to love me, if you refuse to open your eyes to a little reasonable truth.'

But she would not admit it; she interrupted each sentence that came from him with protests full of vehemence and stupefaction: I! I! It is I whom you accuse! I tell you that you no longer love me, and you dare to assert that I am losing my love for you!' Then, casting aside all restraint, revealing the innermost thoughts that haunted her day by day, she continued: 'Ah! how happy are the women whose husbands share their faith! I see some in church who are always accompanied by their husbands. How delightful it must be for husband and wife to place themselves conjointly in the hands of God! Those homes are blessed, they indeed have but one soul, and there is no felicity that heaven does not shower on them!'

Marc could not restrain a slight laugh, at once very gentle and distressful. 'So now, my poor wife,' he said, 'you think of trying to convert me?'

'What harm would there be in that?' she answered eagerly. 'Do you imagine I do not love you enough to feel frightful grief at the thought of the deadly peril you are in? You do not believe in future punishment, you brave the wrath of heaven; but for my part I pray heaven every day to enlighten you, and I would give—ah! willingly—ten years of my life to be able to open your eyes, and save you from the terrible catastrophes which threaten you. Ah! if you would only love me, and listen to me, and follow me to the land of eternal delight!'

She trembled in his embrace, she glowed with such a fever of superhuman desire that he was thunderstruck, for he had not imagined the evil to be so deep. It was she who catechised him now, who tried to win him to her faith, and he felt ashamed, for was she not doing what he himself ought to have done the very first day—that is, strive to convert her to his own views? He could not help expressing his thoughts aloud, and unluckily he said: 'It is not you yourself who is speaking; you have been given a task full of danger for the happiness of both of us.'

At this she began to lose her temper: 'Why do you wound me like that?' she asked. 'Do you think I am incapable of acting for myself—from personal conviction and affection? Am I senseless, then—so stupid and docile that I can only serve as an instrument? Besides, even if people—who are worthy of all respect, and whose sacred character you disregard—do speak to me about you in a brotherly way which would surprise you—ought you not rather to be moved by it, ought you not to yield to such loving-kindness?... God, who might strike you down, holds out His arms to you ... yet when He makes use of me and my love to lead you back to Him you can only jest and treat me as if I were a foolish little girl repeating a lesson!... Ah! we understand each other no longer, and it is that which grieves me so much!'

While she spoke he felt his fear and desolation increasing. 'That is true,' he repeated slowly, 'we no longer understand one another. Words no longer have the same meaning for us, and every reproach that I address to you, you address to me. Which of us will break away from the other? Which of us loves the other and works for the other's happiness?... Ah! I am the guilty one and I greatly fear that it is too late for me to repair my fault. I ought to have taught you where to find truth and equity.'

At these words, so suggestive of his profession, her rebellion became complete. 'Yes, for you I am always a foolish pupil who knows nothing and whose eyes require to be opened. But it is I who know where truth and justice are to be found. You have not the right to speak those words.'

'Not the right!'

'No; you have plunged into that monstrous error, that ignoble Simon affair, in which your hatred of the Church blinds you and urges you to the worst iniquity. When a man like you goes so far as to override all truth and justice in order to strike and befoul the ministers of religion, it is better to believe that he has lost his senses.'

This time Marc reached the root of the quarrel which Geneviève was picking with him. The Simon case lay beneath everything else, it was that alone which had inspired all the discreet and skilful manœuvring of which he beheld the effects. If his wife were enticed away from him at her relatives' home, if she were employed as a weapon to strike him a deadly blow, it was especially in order that an artisan of truth, a possible justiciary, might be smitten in his person. It was necessary to suppress him, for his destruction alone could ensure the impunity of the real culprits.

His voice trembled with deep grief as he answered: 'Ah! Geneviève, this is more serious. There will be an end to our home if we can no longer agree on so clear and so simple a question. Are you no longer on my side, then, in that painful affair?'

'No, certainly not.'

'You think poor Simon guilty?'

'Why, there is no doubt of it! The reasons you give for asserting his innocence repose on no foundation whatever! I should like you to hear the persons whose purity of life you dare to suspect! And as you fall into such gross error respecting a case in which everything is so evident, a case which is settled beyond possibility of appeal, how can I place the slightest faith in your other notions, your fanciful social system, in which you begin by suppressing religion?'

He had taken her in his arms again, and was holding her in a tight embrace. Ah! she was right. Their slowly increasing rupture had originated in their divergence of views on that question of truth and justice, in reference to which others had managed to poison her understanding. 'Listen,

Geneviève,' he said; 'there is only one truth, one justice. You must listen to me, and our agreement will restore our peace.'

'No, no!'

'But, Geneviève, you must not remain in such darkness when I see light all around me; it would mean separation forever.'

'No, no, let me be! You tire me; I won't even listen.'

She wrenched herself from his embrace and turned her back upon him. He vainly sought to clasp her again, kissing her and whispering gentle words; she would not move, she would not even answer. A chill swept down on the conjugal couch, and the room seemed black as ink, dolorously lifeless, as if the misfortune which was coming had already annihilated everything.

From that time forward Geneviève became more nervous and ill-tempered. Much less consideration was now shown for her husband at her grandmother's house; he was attacked in her presence in an artfully graduated manner, as by degrees her affection for him was seen to decline. Little by little he became a public malefactor, one of the damned, a slayer of the God she worshipped. And the rebellion to which she was thus urged re-echoed in her home in bitter words, in an increase of discomfort and coldness. Fresh quarrels arose at intervals, usually at night, when they retired to rest, for in the daytime they saw little of each other, Marc then being busy with his boys and Geneviève being constantly absent, now at church, now at her grandmother's. Thus their life was gradually quite spoilt. The young woman showed herself more and more aggressive, while her husband, so tolerant by nature, in his turn ended by manifesting irritation.

'My darling, I shall want you to-morrow during afternoon lessons,' he said one evening.

'To-morrow? I can't come,' she replied; 'Abbé Quandieu will be expecting me. Besides, you need not rely on me for anything.'

'Won't you help me, then?'

'No, I detest everything you do. Damn yourself if you choose; but I have to think of my salvation.'

'Then each is to go his own way?'

'As you please.'

'Oh! darling, darling, is it you who speak like that? Are they going to change your heart after fogging your mind? So now you are altogether on the side of the corrupters and poisoners?'

'Be quiet, be quiet, you unhappy man! It is your work which is all falsehood and poison. You blaspheme; your justice and your truth are filthy; and it is the devil—yes, the devil—who teaches those wretched children of yours, whom I no longer even pity, for they must be stupid indeed to remain here!'

'My poor darling, how is it possible that you, once so intelligent, can say such foolish things?'

'When a man finds women foolish he leaves them to themselves.'

Thereupon, in his turn losing his temper, Marc, indeed, left her to herself, making no effort to win her back by a loving caress as in former days. It often happened that they were unable to get to sleep; they lay in bed, side by side, with their eyes wide open in the darkness, silent and motionless, as if the little space which separated them had become an abyss.

Marc was particularly afflicted by the growing hatred which Geneviève manifested against his school, against the dear children whom he so passionately strove to teach. At each fresh dispute she expressed herself so bitterly that it seemed as if she became jealous of the little ones when she saw him treat them so affectionately, endeavour so zealously to make them sensible and peaceable. At bottom, indeed, Geneviève's quarrel with Marc had no other cause; for she herself was but a child, one of those who needed to be taught and freed, but who rebelled and clung stubbornly to the errors of the ages. And in her estimation all the affection which her husband lavished on his boys was diverted from herself. As long as he should busy himself with them in such a fatherly fashion, she would be unable to conquer him, carry him away into the divine and rapturous stultification, in which she would fain have seen him fall asleep in her arms. The struggle at last became concentrated on that one point. Geneviève no longer passed the classroom without feeling an inclination to cross herself, like one who was utterly upset by the diabolical work accomplished there, who was irritated by her powerlessness to wrest from such impious courses the man whose bed she still shared.

Months, even years went by, and the battle between Marc and Geneviève grew fiercer. But no imprudent haste was displayed at the home of her relatives, for the Church has all eternity before her to achieve her ends. Besides, leaving on one side that vain marplot, Brother Fulgence, Father Théodose and Father Crabot were too skilled in the manipulation of souls to overlook the necessity of proceeding slowly with a woman of passionate nature, whose mind was an upright one when mysticism did not obscure and pervert it. As long as she should love her husband, as long as there should be no conjugal rupture, the work they had undertaken would not be complete. And it required a long time to uproot and extirpate a great love from a woman's heart and flesh in such wise that it might never grow again. Thus Geneviève was left in the hands of Abbé Quandieu, so that he might gently rock her to sleep before more energetic action was attempted. Meantime, the others contented themselves with watching her. It was a masterpiece of delicate, gradual, but certain spell working.

Another affair helped to disturb Marc's home. He took a great deal of interest in Madame Férou, who had installed herself with her three daughters in a wretched lodging at Maillebois, where she had sought work as a seamstress while awaiting a summons from her husband, the dismissed schoolmaster, who had fled to Brussels to seek employment there. But the wretched man's endeavours had proved fruitless. He had found himself unable even to provide for his own wants; and tortured by separation, exasperated by exile, he had lost his head and returned to Maillebois with the bravado of one whom misery pursues and who can know no worse misfortune than that already befalling him. Denounced on the very next day, he was seized by the military authorities as a deserter, and Salvan had to intervene actively to save him from being incorporated at once in some disciplinary company. He was now in garrison in a little Alpine town, at the other end of France, while his wife and daughters, scarcely possessed of shelter and clothes, often found themselves without bread.

Marc also had exerted himself on Férou's behalf at the time of his arrest. He had then seen him for a few minutes and was unable to forget him. That poor, big, haggard fellow lingered in his mind like the victim, *par excellence*, of social abomination. Doubtless he had made his retention in office impossible, even as Mauraisin said; but how many excuses there were for this shepherd's son who had become a schoolmaster, who had been starved for years, who had been treated with so much scorn on account of his poverty, who had been cast to the most extreme views by his circumstances: he, a man of intelligence and learning, who found himself possessing nothing, knowing not one joy of life, whereas ignorant brutes possessed and enjoyed all around him. And the long iniquity had ended in brutal barrack-life far away from those who were dear to him, and who were perishing of misery.

'Is it not enough to goad one into turning everything upside down?' he had cried to Marc at their brief interview, his eyes flashing while he waved his long bony arms. 'I signed, it's true, a ten years' engagement which exempted me from barrack-life if I gave those ten years to teaching. And it's true also that I gave only eight years, as I was revoked for having said what I thought about the black-frocks' revolting idolatry! But was it I who cancelled my engagement? And after casting me brutally adrift, without any means of subsistence, isn't it monstrous to seize me and claim payment of my old debt to the army, in such wise that my wife and children must remain with nobody to earn a living for them? The eight years I spent in the university penitentiary, where a man who believes in truth is allowed neither freedom of speech nor freedom of action, were not enough for them! They insist on robbing me of two more years, on shutting me up in their gaol of blood and iron, and reducing me to that life of passive obedience which is the necessary apprenticeship for devastation and massacre, the mere thought of which exasperates me! Ah! it's too much. I've given them quite enough of my life, and they will end by maddening me if they ask me for more.'

Alarmed at finding him so excited, Marc tried to calm him by promising to do all he could for his wife and daughters. In two years' time he would be released, and then some position might be found for him, and he would be able to begin his life afresh. But Férou remained gloomy, and growled angry words: 'No, no, I'm done for. I shall never get through those two years quietly. They know it well, and it's to get the chance of killing me like a mad dog that they are sending me yonder.'

Then he inquired who had replaced him at Le Moreux, and on hearing that it was a man named Chagnat, an ex-assistant teacher at Brévannes, a large parish of the region, he began to laugh bitterly. Chagnat, a dusky little man with a low brow and retreating mouth and chin, was the personification of the perfect beadle—not a hypocrite like Jauffre, who made use of religion as a means to advancement, but a shallow-brained bigot, such a dolt indeed as to believe in any nonsensical trash that fell from the priest's lips. His wife, a huge carroty creature, was yet more stupid than himself. And Férou's bitter gaiety increased when he learnt that Mayor Saleur had completely abdicated in favour of that idiot Chagnat, whom Abbé Cognasse employed as a kind of sacristan-delegate to rule the parish on his behalf.

'When I told you long ago,' said Férou, 'that all that dirty gang, the priests, the good Brothers, and the good Sisters, would eat us up and reign here, you wouldn't believe me; you declared that my mind was diseased! Well, now it has come to pass; they are your masters, and you'll see into what a fine mess they will lead you. It disgusts one to be a man: a stray dog is less to be pitied. And as for myself I've had quite enough of it all. I'll bring things to an end if they plague me.'

Nevertheless Férou was sent off to join his regiment, and another three months went by, the wretchedness of his unhappy wife steadily increasing. She, once so fair and pleasant with her bright and fresh round face, now looked twice as old as she really was, aged betimes by hard toil and want. She still found very little work, and spent an entire winter month fireless, almost without bread. To make matters worse, her eldest daughter fell ill with typhoid fever, and lay perishing in the icy garret into which the wind swept through every chink in the door and window. Marc, who in a discreet way had already given alms to the poor woman, at last begged his wife to entrust her with some work.

Although Geneviève spoke of Férou even as those whom she met at her grandmother's house spoke of him, saying that he had blasphemously insulted the Sacred Heart and was a sacrilegist, she felt stirred by the story of his wife's bitter want. 'Yes,' she said to her husband, 'Louise needs a new frock; I have the stuff, and I will take it to that woman.'

'Thank you for her. I will go with you,' Marc replied.

On the following day they repaired together to Madame Férou's sordid lodging, whence her landlord threatened to expel her as she was in arrears with her rent. Her eldest daughter was now near her death; and when the Froments arrived she herself and her two younger girls were sobbing in heartrending fashion amid the fearful disorder of the place. For a moment Marc and Geneviève remained standing there, amazed and unable to understand the situation.

'You haven't heard it, you haven't heard it, have you?' Madame Férou at last exclaimed. 'Well, it's done now; they are going to kill him. Ah! he guessed it; he said that those brigands would end by having his skin.'

She went on speaking in a disjointed fashion amid her sobs, and Marc was thus able to extract from her the distressful story. Férou, as was inevitable, had turned out a very bad soldier, and unfavourably noted by his superiors, treated with the utmost harshness as a revolutionary, he had carried a quarrel with his corporal so far as to rush on the latter and kick and pommel him. For this he had been court-martialled, and they were now about to send him to a military *bagnio* in Algeria, where he would be drafted into one of those disciplinary companies, among which the abominable tortures of the old ages are still practised.

'He will never come back, they will murder him!' his wife continued in a fury. 'He wrote to bid me good-bye; he knows that he will soon be killed.... And what shall I do? What will become of my poor children? Ah! the brigands, the brigands!'

Marc listened, sorely grieved, unable to think of a word of consolation, whereas Geneviève began to show signs of impatience. 'But, my dear Madame Férou,' she exclaimed, 'why should they kill your husband? The officers of our army are not in the habit of killing their men. You increase your own distress by your unjust thoughts.'

'They are brigands, I tell you!' the unhappy woman repeated with growing violence. 'What! my poor Férou starved for eight years, discharging the most ungrateful duties, and he is taken for another two years and treated like a brute beast, simply because he spoke like a sensible man! And now what was bound to happen has happened; he is sent to the galleys, where they'll end by murdering him after dragging him from agony to agony! No, no, I won't have it! I'll go and tell them that they are all a band of brigands—brigands!'

Marc endeavoured to calm her. He, all kindliness and equity, was shocked by such excessive social iniquity. But what could those on whom it recoiled, the wife and children, do, crushed as they were beneath the millstone of tragic fate? 'Be reasonable,' said he. 'We will try to do something; we will not forsake you.'

But Geneviève had become icy cold. That wretched home where the mother was wringing her hands, where the poor puny girls were sobbing and lamenting, no longer inspired her with any pity. She no longer even saw the eldest daughter, wrapped in the shreds of a blanket and looking so ghastly as she gazed at the scene with dilated, expressionless eyes, unable even to weep, such was her weakness. Erect and rigid, still carrying the little parcel formed of the stuff for Louise's new frock, the young woman slowly said: 'You must place yourself in the hands of God. Cease to offend Him, for He might punish you still more.'

A laugh of terrible scorn came from Madame Férou: 'Oh! God is too busy with the rich to pay attention to the poor!' she cried. 'It was in His name that we were reduced to this misery, it is in His name that they are going to murder my poor husband!'

At this Geneviève was carried away by anger: 'You blaspheme! You deserve no help!' said she. 'If you had only shown a little religious feeling, I know persons who would have helped you already.'

'But I ask you for nothing, madame,' the poor woman answered. 'Yes, I know that help has been refused me because I do not go to confession. Even Abbé Quandieu, who is so charitable, does not dare to include me among his poor.... But I am not a hypocrite, I simply endeavour to earn my bread by work.'

'Well, then, apply for work to the wretched madmen who regard the priests and the officers as brigands!'

And thereupon Geneviève hurried away in a passion, carrying with her the stuff for her daughter's frock. Marc was obliged to follow her, though he quivered with indignation. And halfway down the stairs he could restrain himself no longer. 'You have just done a bad action!' he exclaimed.

'How?'

'How? A God of kindness would be charitable to all. Your God of wrath and punishment is but a monstrous phantasy.... It is not necessary that one should humble oneself to deserve assistance, it is sufficient that one should suffer.'

'No, no! Those who sin deserve their sufferings! Let them suffer if they persist in impiety. My duty is to do nothing for them.'

That same evening, when they were alone, the quarrel began afresh, and Marc, on his side, for the first time became violent, unable as he was to forgive Geneviève's lack of charity. Hitherto he had fancied that her mind alone was threatened, but was it not evident now that her heart also would be spoilt? And that night irreparable words were spoken, husband and wife realised what an abyss had been dug between them by invisible hands. Then both relapsed into silence in the black room full of grief and pain, and on the morrow they did not exchange a word.

Moreover, a source of constant disputes, one which was bound to make rupture inevitable, had now sprung up. Louise would be soon ten years old, and the question of sending her to Abbé Quandieu's Catechism classes, in order that she might be prepared for her first Communion, presented itself. Marc, after begging Mademoiselle Rouzaire to exempt his daughter from all religious exercises, had noticed that the schoolmistress took no account of his request, but crammed the child with orisons and canticles as she did with her other pupils. But he was obliged to close his eyes to it, for he realised that the schoolmistress was only too anxious to have a chance of appealing to Geneviève on the subject in order to create trouble in his home. When the Catechism question arose, however, he desired to act firmly, and watched for an opportunity to have a decisive explanation with Geneviève. That opportunity presented itself naturally enough on the day when Louise, returning from her lessons, said to her mother in her father's presence: 'Mamma, Mademoiselle Rouzaire told me to ask you to see Abbé Quandieu, so that he may put my name down for his Catechism class.'

'All right, my dear, I will go to see him to-morrow.'

Marc, who was reading, quickly raised his head: 'Excuse me, my dear, but you will not go to Abbé Quandieu.'

'Why not?'

'It is simple enough. I do not wish Louise to follow the Catechism lessons because I do not wish her to make her first Communion.'

Geneviève did not immediately lose her temper, but laughed as if with ironical compassion: 'You are out of your senses, my friend,' said she. 'Not make her first Communion indeed! Why in that case how would you find a husband for her? What a casteless, shameless position you would give her throughout her life! Besides, you allowed her to be baptised, you allowed her to learn her Bible history and prayers, so it is illogical on your part to forbid the Catechism and the Communion.'

Marc also kept his temper for the moment, and answered quietly: 'You are right, I was weak, and for that very reason I am resolved to be weak no longer. I showed all tolerance for your belief as long as the child remained quite young, and hung about your skirts. A daughter, it is said, ought to belong more particularly to her mother, and I am willing that it should be so until the time comes when the question of the girl's moral life, her whole future, presents itself. Surely the father then has a right to intervene?'

Geneviève waved her hand impatiently and her voice began to tremble as she answered: 'I wish Louise to follow the Catechism lessons, you don't wish her to do so. If we have equal rights over the child we may go on disputing for ever without reaching a solution. What I desire seems to you idiotic, and what you desire appears to me abominable.'

'Oh! what I desire, what I desire! My desire simply is that my daughter shall not be prevented from exercising her own free will later on.... The question now is to profit by her childishness in order to deform her mind and heart, poison her with lies, and render her for ever incapable of becoming human and sensible. And that is what I desire to prevent. But I do not wish to impose my will on her, I simply wish to ensure her the free exercise of her will at a later date.'

'But how do you provide for that? What is to be done with this big girl?'

'It is only necessary to let her grow up and to open her eyes to every truth. When she is twenty she will decide who is right—you or I; and if she should then think it sensible and logical she will revert to the Catechism and make her first Communion.'

At this Geneviève exploded: 'You are really mad! You say such absurd things before the child that I feel ashamed of you!'

Marc also lost patience. 'Absurd, my poor wife? It is your notions that are absurd! And I won't have my child's mind perverted with such absurdities.'

'Be quiet! be quiet!' she cried. 'You don't know what you wrench from me when you speak like that! Yes, you tear away all my love for you, all our happiness, which I should still like to save!... But how are we to agree if words no longer have the same meaning for us, if what you declare to be absurd is for me the divine and the eternal?... And is not your fine logic at fault? How can Louise choose between your ideas and mine if you now prevent me from having her instructed as I desire?... I do not prevent you from telling her whatever you wish, but I must be free to take her to the Catechism class.'

Marc was already weakening: 'I know the theory,' said he. 'The child enlightened by both the father and the mother, with the right of choosing between their views later on. But is that right left intact when a full course of religious training, aggravating the child's long Catholic heredity, deprives her of all power of thinking and acting freely? The father, who is so imperfectly armed, can do little when he talks truth and sense to a girl whose senses and whose heart are disturbed by others. And when she has grown up amid the pomps of the Church, its terrifying mysteries and its mystical absurdities, it is too late for her to revert to a little sense—her mind has been warped for ever.'

'If you have your right as a father,' Geneviève retorted violently, 'I have my right as a mother. You are not going to take my daughter from me when she is only ten years old and still has so much need of me. It would be monstrous! I am an honest woman, and I mean to make Louise an honest woman too.... She shall go to the Catechism class, and, if necessary, I myself will take her!'

Marc, who had risen from his chair, made a furious gesture of protest, but he had strength enough to restrain the violent, the supreme words which would have precipitated immediate rupture. What could he say, what could he do? As usual, he recoiled from the fearful prospect of seeing his home destroyed, his happiness changed into hourly torture. He still loved that woman who showed herself so narrow-minded and particularly so stubborn; there still lingered on his lips the taste of hers; and he could not forget, he could not obliterate, the happy days of their early married life, the powerful bond then formed between them, that child who was the flesh of their flesh, and now the cause of their quarrels. Like many others before him he felt he was driven into a corner, whence he could not extricate himself unless he took to brutal courses—tore the child from her mother's arms, and plunged the house into desolation and commotion every day. And there was too much gentleness, too much kindness, in his nature; he lacked the cold energy that was requisite for a struggle in which his own heart and the hearts of those he loved must bleed. On that field then he was foredoomed to defeat.

Louise had listened in silence, without moving, to the dispute between her father and mother. For some time past, whenever she had seen them thus at variance, her large brown eyes had glanced from one to the other with an expression of sad and increasing surprise.

'But, papa,' she now said, amid the painful silence which had fallen, 'why don't you wish me to go to the Catechism class?'

She was very tall for her age, and had a calm and gentle face, in which the features of the Duparques and the Froments were blended. Though she was still only a child, she displayed keen intelligence, and a thirst for information which constantly impelled her to ply her father with questions. And she worshipped him, and showed also great affection for her mother, who attended to all her wants with a kind of loving passion.

'So you think, papa,' she resumed, 'that if things which are not reasonable are told me at the Catechism class I shall accept them?'

Marc, in spite of his emotion, could not help smiling. 'Reasonable or not,' said he, 'you must of necessity accept them.'

'But you will explain them to me?'

'No, my dear; they are, and must remain, unexplainable.'

'But you explain to me everything I ask you when I come back from Mademoiselle Rouzaire's and haven't understood some lesson.... It is thanks to you that I am often the first of my class.'

'If you came back from Abbé Quandieu's there would be nothing for me to explain to you,' Marc answered, 'for the essential characteristic of the pretended truths of the Catechism is that they are not accessible to our reason.'

'Ah! how funny!'

For a moment Louise remained silent, in meditation, her glance wandering far away. Then, still with a pensive expression on her face, she slowly gave utterance to her thoughts. 'It's funny; when things haven't been explained to me and I don't understand them I recollect nothing about them, it is as if they didn't exist. I close my eyes and see nothing. Everything is black. And then, however much I may try, I'm the last of the class.'

She looked charming with her serious little face, well balanced as she already was, going instinctively towards all that was good, clear, and sensible. Whenever an attempt was made to force into her head things whose sense escaped her, or which seemed to her to be wrong, she smiled in a quiet way and passed them by.

But Geneviève now intervened, saying with some irritation, 'If your father cannot explain the Catechism to you I will do so.'

At this Louise immediately ran to kiss her mother as if she feared she had offended her: 'That's it, mamma, you will hear me my lessons. You know that I always try my best to understand.' And, turning towards her father, she gaily resumed, 'You see, papa, you may as well let me go to the Catechism, particularly as you say yourself that one ought to learn everything, so that one may be the better able to judge and choose.'

Then, once again, Marc gave way, having neither the strength nor the means to act otherwise. He reproached himself with his weakness; but such was his craving for affection that it was impossible for him to be otherwise than weak when he thought of his devastated home where the struggle each day became more painful.

The rupture was soon to be precipitated, however, by a final incident. Years had elapsed since Marc's arrival at Maillebois, and there had been all sorts of changes among his pupils. Sébastien Milhomme, his favourite, now fifteen years of age, was by his advice preparing himself for admission into the Training College of Beaumont, having secured his elementary certificate already in his twelfth year. Four other boys had left the school with similar certificates—the two Doloirs and the twin Savins. Auguste Doloir had now embraced his father's calling as a mason, while his brother Charles had been apprenticed to a locksmith. As for Savin, he had declined to follow Marc's advice and make schoolmasters of his sons, for he did not wish to see them starve, said he, in an ungrateful calling which everybody held in contempt. So he had proudly placed Achille with a process-server and was looking about him for some petty employment which would suit Philippe.

Meantime, the hard-headed Fernand Bongard had quietly returned to his father's farm to till the ground, having failed to gain a certificate, though in Marc's hands he had acquired more understanding than his parents possessed. As for the girls who had quitted Mademoiselle Rouzaire, Angèle Bongard, who was more intelligent than her brother, had duly carried a certificate to the farm, where, like the shrewd ambitious young person she was, quite capable of keeping accounts, she dreamt of improving her position. Then Hortense Savin, still without a certificate at sixteen years of age, had become a very pretty brunette, extremely devout and sly. She had remained a Handmaiden of the Virgin, and her father dreamt of a fine marriage for her, though there were rumours of a mysterious seduction, the consequences of which she each day found it more difficult to hide.

Of course several new boys had come to Marc's school, replacing their elders there. There was another little Savin, Jules, whom Marc remembered having seen as an infant at the time of the Simon case; and there was another little Doloir, Léon, born subsequent to the affair, and now nearly seven years old. Later on the children's children would be coming to the school, and if Marc were left at his post perhaps he would teach them also, thus facilitating another step to humanity, ever on the march towards increase of knowledge.

But Marc was particularly concerned about one of his new boys, one whom he had greatly desired to have at the school. This was little Joseph, Simon's son, who had now almost completed his eleventh year. For a long time Marc had not dared to expose him to the taunts and blows of the other boys. Then, thinking that their passions had calmed down sufficiently, he had made the venture, applying to Madame Simon and the Lehmanns, and promising them that he would keep a good watch over the lad. For three years now he had had Joseph in the school, and, after defending him against all sorts of vexations, had prevailed on the other boys to treat him with some good fellowship. Indeed, he even made use of the lad as a living example when seeking to inculcate principles of tolerance, dignity, and kindness.

Joseph was a very handsome boy, in whom his mother's beauty was blended with his father's intelligence; and the dreadful story of his father's fate, with which it had been necessary to acquaint him, seemed to have ripened him before his time. Usually grave and reserved, he studied with a sombre ardour, intent on being always the first of his class, as if, by that triumph, to raise himself above all outrage. His dream, his express desire, which Marc encouraged, was to become a schoolmaster, for in this he boyishly pictured a kind of *revanche* and rehabilitation. No doubt it was Joseph's fervour, the passionate gravity of that clever and handsome boy, which the more particularly struck little Louise, whose senior he was by nearly three years. At all events she became his great friend, and they were well pleased whenever they found themselves together.

At times Marc kept Joseph after lessons, and at times also his sister Sarah came to fetch him. Then, if Sébastien Milhomme, as was sometimes the case, happened to be at Marc's, a delightful hour was spent. The four children agreed so well that they never quarrelled. Sarah, whom her mother feared to confide to others as she did her boy, was, at ten years of age, a most charming child, gentle and loving; and Sébastien, five years her elder, treated her with the playful affection of an elder brother. Geneviève alone manifested violent displeasure when the four children happened to meet in her rooms. She found in this another cause for anger with her husband. Why had he brought those Jews into their home? There was no need for her daughter to compromise herself by associating with the children of that horrid criminal who had been sent to the galleys! Thus this also helped to bring about quarrels in the home.

At last came the fated catastrophe. One evening, when the four young people were playing together after lessons, Sébastien suddenly felt ill. He staggered as if intoxicated, and Marc had to take him to his mother's. On the morrow the boy was unable to leave his bed, a terrible attack of typhoid fever prostrated him, and for three weeks his life hung in the balance. It was a frightful time for his mother, Madame Alexandre, who remained at his bedside, no longer setting foot in the shop downstairs. Moreover, since the Simon affair she had gradually withdrawn from it, leaving her sister-in-law, Madame Edouard, to conduct the business in accordance with their joint interests. As a matter of fact, Madame Edouard, who was the man in their partnership, was designated for the directorship by the triumph of the clerical party. The custom of the secular school was sufficiently insured by the presence of Madame Alexandre behind her, and for her own part she intended to increase her business among the devotees of the town with the help of her son Victor, who had lately left the Brothers' school.

He was now a big, squarely-built youth of seventeen, with a large head, a harsh face, and fierce eyes. He had failed to secure an elementary certificate, having always shown himself an execrable pupil; and he now dreamt of enlisting and becoming a general as in the old days, when he had played at war with his cousin Sébastien, taken him prisoner, and pommelled him passionately. Meantime, as he was not old enough for soldiering, he lived in idleness, making his escape from the shop as often as possible—for he hated having to stand behind a counter and sell paper and pens—and roaming through Maillebois in the company of his old schoolfellow Polydor, the son of Souquet the road-mender, and the nephew of Pélagie, Madame Duparque's servant.

Polydor, a pale and artful youth, whose taste for idleness was extraordinary, desired to become an Ignorantine by way of flattering the inclinations of his aunt, from whom he thereby extracted little presents. Moreover, by embracing this religious calling he would not have to break stones on the roads as his father did, and, in particular, he would escape barrack-life, the thought of which quite horrified him. Though in other respects Victor and Polydor had different tastes, they were in full agreement as to the delight of roaming about from morn till night with their hands in their pockets, to say nothing of their goings on with the little hussies of the factory quarter of the town, whom they met in the fields near the Verpille. In this wise, Victor being always out and about, and Madame Alexandre remaining beside her son, Madame Edouard, since Sébastien had fallen so seriously ill, found herself quite without assistance in the shop, where she busied herself with her customers and gaily counted up her takings, which were often large.

Marc went every evening to ascertain the condition of his pupil, and thus he became a daily spectator of a heartrending drama—the bitter grief of a mother who saw death taking her son a little further from her every hour. That gentle, fair, pale-faced Madame Alexandre, who had loved her husband passionately, had been leading a cloistered life, as it were, ever since his death, all her restrained passion going to that son of hers, who was fair and gentle like herself. Fondled, almost spoilt by that loving mother, Sébastien regarded her with a kind of filial idolatry, as if she were a divine mother whom he could never requite for all her delightful gifts. They were united by a strong, a powerful bond of tender affection, one of those infinite affections in which two beings mingle and blend to such a point that neither can quit the other without wrenching away his or her heart.

When Marc reached the little dark, close room over the stationery shop, he often found Madame Alexandre forcing back her tears and striving to smile at her son, who lay there already emaciated and burning with fever.

'Well, Sébastien, are you better to-day?' the master would ask.

'Oh! no, Monsieur Froment, I'm no better at all—no better at all.'

He could scarcely speak, his voice was faint, his breath came short. But the red-eyed, shuddering mother exclaimed gaily: 'Don't listen to him, Monsieur Froment, he is much better, we shall pull him through it.'

When, however, she had escorted the schoolmaster to the landing, and stood there with him after closing the door of the room, she broke down.

'Ah! God, he is lost, my poor child is lost! Is it not abominable, so strong and handsome as he was! His poor face is reduced to nothing; he has only his eyes left! Ah! God, God, I feel I shall die with him.'

But she stifled her cries, roughly wiped away her tears, and put on her smile once more before returning to the chamber of suffering where she spent hours and hours, without sleep, without help, ever fighting against death.

One evening Marc found her sobbing on her knees beside the bed, her face close pressed to the sheets. Her son could no longer hear or see her. Since the previous night he had been overpowered by his malady, seized with delirium. And now that he had neither ears to hear her nor eyes to see her, she abandoned herself to her frightful grief, and cried it aloud: 'My child, my child! What have I done that my child should be stolen from me?

So good a son, who was all my heart as I was his! What can I have done then? What can I have done?'

She rose and, grasping Marc's hands, pressed them wildly. 'Tell me, monsieur, you who are just,' said she. 'Is it not impossible to suffer so much, to be stricken like this if one be free from all blame?... It would be monstrous to be punished when one has done no wrong. Is it not so? This, then, can only be an expiation, and if that were true, ah! if I knew, if I knew it were so!...'

She seemed a prey to some horrible struggle. For some days past anguish had been making her restless. Yet she did not speak out that evening; it was only on the morrow that, on Marc's arrival, she hastened towards him, as if carried away by an eager desire to have it all over. In the bed near her lay Sébastien, scarce able to breathe.

'Listen, Monsieur Froment,' said she, 'I must confess myself to you. The doctor has just left, my son is dying, only a prodigy can save him.... And now my fault stifles me. It seems to me that it is I who am killing my son—I who am punished by his death for having made him speak falsely long ago, and for having clung so stubbornly to that falsehood later on, in order to have peace and quietness in my home, when another, an innocent man, was suffering the worst torture.... Ah! for many, many days the struggle has been going on within me, lacerating my heart!'

Marc listened, amazed, not daring as yet to give a meaning to her words.

'You remember, Monsieur Froment,' she resumed, 'you remember that unhappy man Simon, the schoolmaster who was condemned for the murder of little Zéphirin. For more than eight years he has been in penal servitude, and you have often told me of all he suffered yonder, horrible things which made me feel quite ill.... I should have liked to speak out—yes, I swear it! I was often on the point of relieving my conscience, for remorse haunted me so dreadfully.... But cowardice came over me; I thought of my son's peace, of all the worries I should cause him.... Ah! how stupid, how foolish I was; I remained silent for the sake of his happiness, and now death is taking him from me—taking him, it's certain, because I wrongly remained silent!'

She paused, gesticulating wildly, as if Justice, the eternal, were falling on her like a thunderbolt.

'And so, Monsieur Froment, I must relieve my mind. Perhaps there is still time—perhaps Justice will take pity on me if I repair my fault.... You remember the writing slip, and the search which was made for another copy of it. On the day after the crime Sébastien told you that he had seen one in the hands of his cousin Victor, who had brought it from the Brothers' school; and that was true. But that same day we were frightened to such a point that my sister-in-law compelled my son to tell a falsehood by saying that he had made a mistake.... A long while afterwards I found that slip forgotten in an old copybook which Victor had given to Sébastien, and later Sébastien, who felt worried by his falsehood, acknowledged it to you. When he came home and told me of his confession, I was filled with alarm, and in my turn I lied—first of all to him, saying, in order to quiet his scruples, that the paper no longer existed, as I had destroyed it. And that assuredly is the wrong-doing for which I am punished. The paper still exists; I never dared to burn it; some remaining honesty restrained me. And here, here it is, Monsieur Froment! Rid me of it, rid me of that abominable paper, for it is that which has brought misfortune and death into the house!'

She hastened to a wardrobe, and from under a pile of linen she drew Victor's old copybook, in which the writing slip had been slumbering for eight years past. Marc looked at it, thunderstruck. At last, there was the document which he had believed to be destroyed, there was the 'new fact' which he had sought so long! The slip he held appeared to be in all respects similar to the one which had figured at the trial. There were the words '*Aimez vous les uns les autres*'; there was the illegible paraph recalling the one which the experts had pretended to identify with Simon's initials; and it was difficult to contend that the slip had not come from the Brothers' school, for Victor himself had copied it in his book, a whole page of which was filled with the words inscribed on it. But all at once Marc was dazed. There, in the left-hand corner of the slip—the corner missing in the copy which had been used in evidence at the trial—was an imprint, quite plain and quite intact, of the stamp with which the Brothers stamped everything belonging to their school. A sudden light was thus shed on the affair: somebody had torn away the corner of the copy found in Zéphirin's room in order to annihilate the stamp and put Justice off the scent.

Quivering with excitement, carried away by gratitude and sympathy, Marc grasped the poor mother's hands. 'Ah, madame,' he exclaimed, 'you have done a great and worthy action, and may death take pity and restore your son to you!'

At that moment they perceived that Sébastien, who had given no sign of consciousness since the previous evening, had just opened his eyes and was looking at them. They felt profoundly stirred. The ailing lad evidently recognised Marc, but he was not yet free from delirium. 'What beautiful sunshine, Monsieur Froment,' he stammered in a faint voice. 'I'll get up and you'll take me with you. I'll help you to give lessons.'

His mother ran to him and kissed him wildly. 'Make haste to get well, make haste to get well, my boy! Neither of us must ever more tell a falsehood, we must be always good and just!'

As Marc quitted the room he found that Madame Edouard, hearing a noise, had come upstairs. The door having remained open she had witnessed the whole scene, and had seen him place her son's old copybook and the slip in the inner pocket of his coat. She followed him down the stairs in silence, but when they reached the shop she stopped him, saying, 'I am in despair, Monsieur Froment. You must not judge us severely; we are only two poor lone women, and find it difficult indeed to earn a little competence for our old age.... I don't ask you to give me that paper back. You are going to make use of it, and I cannot oppose you: I understand it fully. Only this is a real catastrophe for us.... And again, do not think me a bad woman if I try to save our little business.'

Indeed she was not a bad woman; it merely happened that she had no faith, no passion, apart from the prosperity of that humble stationery business. She had already reflected that if the secular school should gain the day, it would merely be necessary for her to retire into the background and allow Madame Alexandre to direct the shop. Nevertheless, this was hardly a pleasant prospect, given her business instincts and her fondness for domineering over others. So she strove to lighten the catastrophe as far as possible.

'You might content yourself with utilising the slip, without producing my son's copybook,' said she. 'Besides, it has just occurred to me that you might arrange a story and say, for instance, that I happened to find the slip and gave it to you. That would show us in a suitable *rôle*, and we could then openly pass over to your side, with the certainty that you would be victorious.'

In spite of his emotion Marc could not refrain from smiling. 'It is, I think, madame, easiest and most honourable to tell the truth,' said he. 'Your *rôle* will nevertheless remain praiseworthy.'

At this she seemed to feel somewhat reassured. 'Really,' she replied, 'you think so? Of course I ask nothing better than that the truth should become known if we do not have to suffer from it.'

Marc had complaisantly taken the copybook and the slip from his pocket in order to show her exactly what he was carrying away. And she was telling him that she fully recognised both book and slip when, all at once, her son Victor came in from some escapade, accompanied by his friend Polydor Souquet. While twisting about and laughing over some prank known to themselves alone, the two young fellows glanced at the copy-slip, and Polydor at once expressed the liveliest surprise.

'Hallo!' he exclaimed, 'the paper!'

But when Marc quickly raised his head, struck as he was by that exclamation, and divining that a little more of the truth lurked behind it, the youth reassumed his usual sleepy, hypocritical expression and tried to recall his words.

'What paper? Do you know it, then?' Marc asked him.

'I? No.... I said the paper because—because it is a paper.'

Marc could draw nothing further from him. As for Victor, he continued to sneer as if he were amused to find that old affair cropping up once more. Ah! yes, the copy-slip which he had brought home from school one day long ago, and which that little fool Sébastien had made such a fuss about! But Madame Edouard still felt ashamed, and when Marc withdrew she accompanied him outside to beg him to do all he could to spare them worry. She had just thought of General Jarousse, their cousin, who would certainly not be pleased if the affair were revived. He had formerly done them the great honour to call on them and explain that when one's country might suffer from the truth being made known it was infinitely preferable and far more glorious to tell a lie. And if General Jarousse should be angered, whatever would she do with her son Victor, who relied on his relative's protection to become a general in his turn?

That evening Marc was to dine at Madame Duparque's, whither he still repaired at times, as he was unwilling that Geneviève should always go alone. Polydor's exclamation still haunted him, for he felt that the truth lurked behind it; and it so happened that when he reached the ladies' house, with Geneviève and Louise, he caught sight of the young fellow whispering eagerly to his aunt Pélagie in the kitchen. Moreover, the ladies' greeting was so frigid that Marc divined in it some threat. During the last few years Madame Berthereau, Geneviève's mother, had been declining visibly, ever in an ailing state, full also of a kind of despairing sadness amid her resignation. But Madame Duparque, the grandmother, though she was now seventy-one, remained combative, terrible, implacable in her faith. In order that Marc might fully understand for what exceptional reasons she thought it right to receive him, she never invited anybody else when he dined at her house. By this course she hoped also to make him understand that his position was that of a pariah, and that it was impossible to ask honest folk to meet him.

That evening, then, as on previous occasions, silence and embarrassment reigned during the meal, and by the hostile demeanour of the others, and particularly by the brusqueness of Pélagie, who served at table, Marc became fully convinced that some storm was about to burst on him. Until the dessert was served, however, Madame Duparque restrained herself like a *bourgeoise* intent on playing her part as mistress of the house correctly. At last, when Pélagie came in with some apples and pears, she said to her: 'You may keep your nephew to dinner, I give you permission.'

The old servant in her scolding, aggressive voice replied: 'Ah! the poor boy needs to recruit himself after the violence that was done him this afternoon.'

At this Marc suddenly understood everything. The ladies had been made acquainted with his discovery of the copy-slip by Polydor, who, for some reason which remained obscure, had hastened to tell everything to his aunt.

'Oh, oh!' said Marc, who could not help laughing, 'who was it that wanted to do violence to Polydor? Was it I, by chance, when the dear boy ventured to bamboozle me so pleasantly by feigning stupidity at Mesdames Milhommes' this afternoon?'

Madame Duparque, however, would not allow such a serious matter to be treated in that ironical fashion. She proceeded to unbosom herself without any show of anger, but in that rigid, cutting manner of hers which suffered no reply. Was it possible that the husband of her dear Geneviève still thought of reviving the abominable affair of that man Simon, that vile assassin, who had been so justly condemned, who deserved no pity whatever, and who ought indeed to have been guillotined? True, there was a monstrous legend of his innocence which evil-minded folk hoped to make use of in order to shake religion and hand France over to the Jews. And now, after obstinately searching among all that filth, Marc pretended that he had found the proof, the famous new fact, which had been announced so many times already. A fine proof indeed, a strip of paper, which had come nobody knew whence nor how, the invention of a pack of children who either lied or were mistaken!

'Grandmother,' Marc quietly answered, 'it was agreed that we should not speak of those matters any more. I have not ventured to make the slightest allusion to them; it is you who begin again. But what good can a dispute do? My conviction is absolute.'

'And you know the real culprit, and you intend to denounce him to justice?' asked the old lady, quite beside herself.

'Certainly.'

At this Pélagie, who was beginning to clear away, could not restrain herself. 'In any case it isn't Brother Gorgias, I can answer for that!' she suddenly cried.

Marc, enlightened by these words, turned towards her. 'Why do you say that?' he asked.

'Because on the evening of the crime Brother Gorgias accompanied my nephew Polydor to his father's, on the road to Jonville, and got back to the school before eleven o'clock. Polydor and other witnesses testified to that at the trial.'

Marc was still gazing fixedly at the old woman, but his mind was busy at work. That which he had long suspected was becoming a moral certainty. He could picture the Brother accompanying Polydor, then returning homeward, pausing before Zéphirin's open window, and talking to the boy. At last he climbed over the low window bar, the better perhaps to see the pictures which the lad had set out on his table. Then, however, came the horrid impulse, abominable madness... and, the child strangled, the murderer fled by the window, which he still left wide open. It was from his own pocket that he had taken that copy of *Le Petit Beaumontais* to use it as a gag, never noticing in his perturbation that the copy-slip was with the newspaper. And on the morrow, when the crime was discovered, it was Father Philibin, who, finding himself unable to destroy the slip, as Mignot had seen it, had been obliged to content himself with tearing away the corner on which the stamp was impressed, thus at all events removing all positive proof of the place whence the slip had come.

Slowly and gravely Marc answered Pélagie: 'Brother Gorgias is the culprit, everything proves it, and I swear it is so!'

Indignant protests arose around the table. Madame Duparque was stifling with indignation. Madame Berthereau, whose mournful eyes went from her daughter to her son-in-law, whose rupture she sorely dreaded, made a gesture of supreme despair. And while little Louise, who paid great attention to her father's words, remained there quietly, never stirring, Geneviève sprang to her feet and quitted the table, saying:

'You would do better to hold your tongue! It will soon be quite impossible for me to remain near you: you will end by making me hate you!'

Later that same evening, when Louise had gone to sleep and the husband and the wife also lay in bed, there came a moment of profound silence in their dark room. Since dinner neither had spoken to the other. But Marc was always the first to try to make friends, for he could not bear the suffering which their quarrels brought him. Now, however, when he gently sought to embrace Geneviève, she nervously pushed him away, quivering as if with repulsion.

'No: let me be!'

Hurt by her manner, he did not insist. And the silence fell heavily again. At last she resumed: 'There is one thing I have not yet told you.... I believe that I am *enceinte*.'

At this, full of happy emotion, her husband drew near to her again, anxious to press her to his heart. 'Oh! my dear, dear wife, what good news! Now we shall indeed belong to each other once more.'

But she freed herself from his clasp with even more impatience than before, as if his presence near her brought her real suffering. 'No, no, let me be,' she repeated; 'I am not well. I sha'n't be able to sleep; it fidgets me to feel you stirring near me.... It will be better to have two beds if things go on like this.'

Not another word passed between them. They lapsed into silence, speaking neither of the Simon affair nor of the tidings which Geneviève had so abruptly announced. Only the sound of their heavy breathing was to be heard in the dark and lifeless room. Neither was asleep, but neither could penetrate the other's anxious, painful thoughts; it was as if they inhabited two different worlds, parted by a distance of many thousand leagues. And vague sobs seemed to come from far away, from the very depths of the black and dolorous night, bewailing the death of their love.

CHAPTER IV

After a few days' reflection Marc made up his mind and requested David to meet him one evening at the Lehmanns' in the Rue du Trou.

For nearly ten years the Lehmanns had been living in their dim and damp little house, amid public execration. When, as sometimes happened, bands of clericals and anti-Semites came down and threatened the shop, they hastily put up the shutters and continued working by the smoky light of two lamps. All their Maillebois customers, even their co-religionists, having forsaken them, they were dependent on the piece-work they did for Paris clothiers dealing in ready-made goods. And that hard and ill-paid work kept old Lehmann and his mournful wife bent on their board for fourteen hours a day, and yielded scarcely enough money to provide food for themselves, Rachel, and her children, all of whom were huddled there in dismal distress, without a joy or a hope in life. Even now, after so many years, passing pedestrians spat on their doorstep to show how fully they loathed and hated that filthy den, whither, so the legend ran, Simon the murderer had brought Zéphirin's blood, while it was still warm, to use it in some vile deed of witchcraft. And nowadays to that abode of intense wretchedness and deep, cloistered grief came Simon's letters, briefer and more infrequent than formerly, yet still and ever telling the tale of the innocent man's long agony.

Those letters alone had the power of stirring Rachel into life, of drawing her from the torpor and resignation in which she spent most of her days. Her once beautiful countenance was now but a ruin, ravaged by her tears. She lived only for her children: Sarah, whom she still kept beside her, fearing to expose her to the insults of the malicious, and Joseph, whom Marc defended at the school. The dreadful story of their father's fate had long been hidden from them, but it had been necessary to tell them the truth at last, partly in order to spare them much painful doubt and cogitation. Nowadays, whenever a letter arrived from the penal settlement yonder, it was read in their presence; and those bitter trials inculcated virility of nature in them, and helped to ripen their budding minds. After each perusal their mother took them in her arms, repeating that nowhere under the skies was there a more honest, a more noble, a loftier-minded man than their father. She swore to them that he was innocent, she told them of the awful martyrdom he endured, she prophesied to them that he would some day be freed, rehabilitated, and acclaimed; and she asked them to love and revere him when that day should dawn, to encompass him with a worship whose sweetness might enable him to forget his many years of torture.

And yet would the unhappy man live until that day of truth and justice? It was a miracle that he had not succumbed already, among the brutes who crucified him. To survive, he had needed an extraordinary amount of moral energy, the frigid power of resistance, the well-balanced logical temperament with which nature had fortunately endowed him. Still, his last letters gave cause for increasing anxiety, he was evidently at the end of his strength, quite overcome. And Rachel's fears reached such a point that, without pausing to consult anybody, she, usually so languid, repaired one morning to La Désirade to see Baron Nathan, who was then staying there with the Sanglebœufs. She took with her the last letter she had received from her husband in order to show it to the Baron, meaning to beg him—triumphant Jew that he was, one of the gold-kings of the world—to exert his great influence in order to obtain a little pity for the poor, wretched, crucified Jew who was suffering yonder. And she came home in tears, shuddering, as if she had just left some dazzling and fearsome place. She could hardly remember what had happened. The Baron, the bloated renegade, had received her with a stern countenance, as if angered by her audacity. Perhaps it was his daughter, a white-faced, frigid lady, whom she had found with him. She could not tell exactly how they had got rid of her, but it was with words of refusal, such as might have been addressed to a beggar. Then she had found herself outside again, half-blinded by the wealth accumulated at that splendid abode of La Désirade, with its sumptuous reception-rooms, its running waters, and its white statues. And since that fruitless attempt she had relapsed into the mournful, waiting attitude of former days, ever garbed in black, like a living statue of mutely protesting grief in the midst of persecution.

The only person on whom Marc relied in that home of wretchedness and suffering was David, whose mind was so clear, whose heart was so upright and so firm. Ever since the condemnation of Simon Marc had seen him striving, evincing neither impatience, nor weakness, nor despair, despite all the difficulties of his task. Indeed, David's faith remained entire; he was convinced of his brother's innocence, and felt certain that he would some day prove it. He had understood at the outset that he would need some money to achieve his task, and he had arranged his life accordingly. He outwardly resumed the direction of the sand and gravel pits, which he had leased from Baron Nathan, in such wise that everybody believed that he conducted the business personally; but in reality the chief responsibility fell upon his foreman, who was devoted to him. And the profits, being handled prudently, sufficed for David's other work, his real mission, the investigations which he carried on so discreetly. Some people, who believed him to be a miser, accused him of earning large sums of money, and yet giving no help to his sister-in-law, who shared the wretched home of the Lehmanns, where incessant toil led only to a life of privations. At one moment also an attempt was made to dispossess David of his sand and gravel pits, the Sanglebœufs threatening him with an action-at-law, which was evidently prompted by Father Crabot. The Jesuit, indeed, was conscious of the stealthy, underhand efforts which that silent but active man was making, and would have liked to drive him from the district, or at least to cripple his resources. But David fortunately held a thirty years' lease from Baron Nathan, and thus he was still able to carry on the business which ensured him the money he needed.

His principal efforts had been long concentrated on the illegal communication which President Gragnon was said to have made to the jurors in their retiring room, when the proceedings in Simon's trial were over. After interminable inquiries David had collected enough information to picture the scene in its broad lines: the jurors, assailed by certain scruples, had sent for the presiding judge in order to question him about the penalties their verdict might entail; and the judge, in order to silence their scruples, had shown them an old letter of Simon's, which had been placed in his hands a moment previously. This letter, an insignificant note to a friend, acquired importance from the fact that it was followed by a postscript, signed with a paraph identical with the one which figured on the incriminating copy-slip. This singular document, produced at the last moment without the knowledge of the prisoner or his counsel, had assuredly led to the verdict of 'Guilty.' But how was David to establish all this? How could he induce one of the jurors to testify to the facts, the revelation of which would have brought about an immediate revision of the proceedings, particularly if—as David felt convinced—the postscriptum of the letter and its initialling were forgeries? He had long endeavoured to act, through others, on the foreman of the jury, Architect Jacquin, a devout and very upright Catholic; and he believed that he had lately disturbed that man's conscience by acquainting him with the illegality of the judge's communication under the circumstances. If, in addition, he could prove that the postscriptum and the paraph had been forged, Jacquin would speak out.

When Marc repaired to the Rue du Trou to keep the appointment he had made with David, he found the little shop shut, the house quite dark and lifeless. The family had prudently taken refuge in the back parlour, where Lehmann and his wife were working by lamplight; and it was there that the stirring scene took place in the presence of the quivering Rachel and her children, whose eyes were all ablaze.

Before speaking out, however, Marc wished to ascertain what point David had now reached in his investigations.

'Oh! things are moving, but still very, very slowly,' the other answered. 'Jacquin is one of those fair-minded Christians who worship a Deity of love and equity. At one moment I felt alarmed, for I discovered that Father Crabot was bringing the greatest pressure to bear on him through every possible intermediary. But I am now easy on that point—Jacquin will act only as his conscience may direct.... The difficulty is to get at the document in order that it may be examined by experts.'

'But did not Gragnon destroy it?' Marc inquired.

'It seems not. Having shown it to the jurors he did not dare to do so, but simply placed it with the papers in the case, among which it must still be. At least, such is the conviction of Delbos, based on certain information he has obtained. Thus the question is to exhume it from among the records, and it is not easy to devise a plausible motive for doing so.... Nevertheless, we are making progress.' And after a pause David added: 'And you, my friend, have you any good news?'

'Yes, good and great news.'

Then Marc slowly recounted all that had happened: Sébastien's illness, Madame Alexandre's despair, followed by her remorse and terror, which had prompted her to hand him the long-sought duplicate of the copy-slip, on which duplicate one found both the stamp of the Brothers' school and a paraph which undoubtedly represented Brother Gorgias's initials. 'Here it is,' said Marc. 'There, you see, is the stamp, in the very corner which was torn away from the copy found near little Zéphirin's body. We fancied that it might have been bitten off by the victim, but Father Philibin at least had time to tear it off; on that point the recollections of Mignot, my assistant, are precise.... Now, look at the paraph. It is identical with the other which figured at the trial, but it is more legible, and one can fully distinguish Brother Gorgias's initials,[1] that is an F and a G interlaced, which the experts, Masters Badoche and Trabut, with extraordinary aberration, persisted in declaring to be an L and an S, otherwise your brother's initials.... My conviction is now absolute: the culprit is Brother Gorgias, and none other.'

[1] Brother Gorgias = Frère Gorgias.

With passionate eagerness they all stared at the narrow yellow strip of paper produced by Marc, and scrutinised it in the pale lamplight. The old Lehmanns quitted their sewing and thrust their faces forward as if reviving to life. Rachel had emerged from her torpor, and stood there quivering, while the two children, Joseph and Sarah, their eyes aflame, pushed one another in order that they might see the better. Finally David, amid the deep silence of that mourning home, took the paper from Marc and examined it.

'Yes, yes,' he said, 'my conviction is the same as yours. What was suspected has now become certain. Brother Gorgias is the guilty man!'

A long discussion followed; all the facts were recalled in succession, and united in one sheaf. They threw light on each other, and all tended to the same conclusion. Apart from the material proofs which were beginning to come in, there was a moral certainty, the demonstration as it were of a mathematical problem, which reasoning sufficed to solve. No doubt obscurity still hung around a few points, such as the presence of the copy-slip in the Brother's pocket, and the fate of the corner on which the stamp had been impressed. But all the rest seemed certain: Gorgias returning home on the night of the crime, chance bringing him before Zéphirin's open and lighted window, temptation, and afterwards murder; then, on the morrow, chance likewise bringing Father Philibin and Brother Fulgence on the scene in such wise that they became mixed up in the tragedy and were forced to act in order to save one of their fellows. And how plainly did the mutilation of the copy-slip designate the culprit, whose name was virtually proclaimed also by the fierce campaign which had ensued, the great efforts which the Church had made in order to shield him, and cause an innocent man to be sentenced in his stead. Moreover, each day now brought fresh light, and before long the whole huge edifice of falsehood would crumble.

'So that is the end of our wretchedness!' exclaimed old Lehmann, becoming quite gay. 'It will only be necessary to show that paper and Simon will be restored to us.'

The two children were already dancing with delight, repeating in blissful accents: 'Oh! papa will come back! papa will come back!'

But David and Marc remained grave. They knew how difficult and dangerous the situation still was. Questions of the greatest weight and gravity had to be settled: how were they to make use of that newly-discovered document, what course was to be followed in applying for a revision of the trial? Thus Marc answered softly: 'One must think it over, one must wait a little longer.'

At this Rachel, relapsing into tears, stammered amid her sobs: 'Wait! wait for what? For the poor man to die yonder, amid the torture of which he complains?'

Once more the dark little house sank into mourning. All felt that their unhappiness was not yet over. After their keen momentary delight came frightful anxiety as to what the morrow might bring forth.

'Delbos alone can guide us,' said David by way of conclusion. 'If you are willing, Marc, we will go to see him on Thursday.'

'Quite so: call for me on Thursday.'

In ten years Advocate Delbos had risen to a remarkable position at Maillebois. The Simon affair, that compromising case, the brief in which had been prudently declined by all his colleagues and bravely accepted by himself, had decided his future. At that time he had been merely a peasant's son, imbued with some democratic instincts and gifted with eloquence. But, while studying the affair and gradually becoming the impassioned defender of the truth, he had found himself in presence of all the *bourgeois* forces coalescing in favour of falsehood and the maintenance of every social iniquity. And this had ended by making him a militant Socialist, one who felt convinced that the salvation of the country could come solely from the masses. By degrees the whole revolutionary party of the town had grouped itself around him, and at the last elections he had forced a second ballot on the radical Lemarrois, who had been deputy for twenty years. And if Delbos still suffered in his immediate interests from the circumstance that he had defended a Jew charged with every crime, he was gradually rising to a lofty position by the firmness of his faith and the quiet valour of his actions, going forward to victory with gay and virile confidence.

As soon as Marc had shown him the copy-slip obtained from Madame Alexandre, the advocate raised a loud cry of delight: 'At last we hold them!' And turning towards David he added: 'This gives us a second new fact. The first is the letter—a forgery, no doubt—which was illegally communicated to the jury.... We must try to find it among the papers of the case.... And the second is this copy-slip, bearing the stamp of the Brothers' school, and a paraph which is evidently that of Brother Gorgias. It will, I think, be easier and more effective to use this second proof.'

'Then what do you advise me to do?' asked David. 'My idea is to write a letter to the Minister of Justice on behalf of my sister-in-law, a letter formally denouncing Brother Gorgias as the perpetrator of the crime, and applying for the revision of my brother's case.'

Delbos had become thoughtful again. 'That would undoubtedly be the correct course,' said he, 'but it is a delicate matter, and we must not act too hastily.... Let us return for a moment to the illegal communication of that letter, which it will be so difficult for us to prove as long as we cannot induce Architect Jacquin to relieve his conscience. You remember Father

Philibin's evidence—his vague allusion to a paper signed by your brother with a flourish, similar to that on the incriminating copy-slip—a paper about which he would give no precise information—being bound, said he, by confessional secrecy? Well, I am convinced that he was then alluding to the very letter which was placed in Judge Gragnon's hands at the last moment, for which reason, like you, I suspect it to be forged. But these are only suppositions, theories; and we need proofs. Now, if we drop that matter, and, for the time at all events, content ourselves with this duplicate copy of the writing slip, on which the school stamp appears, and on which the initialling is much plainer, we still find ourselves face to face with some puzzling, obscure points. Without lingering too much over the question how it happened that such a slip was in the Brother's pocket at the moment of the crime—a point which it is rather difficult to explain—I am very worried by the disappearance of the corner on which the school stamp must have been impressed; and I should like to find that corner before acting, for I can foresee all sorts of objections which will be raised in opposition to us, in order to throw the affair into a muddle.'

Marc looked at him in astonishment. 'What! find that corner? It would be a wonderful chance if we should do so! We even admitted that it might have been torn away by the victim's teeth.'

'Oh! that is not credible,' Delbos answered. 'Besides, in that case the fragment would have been found on the floor. Nothing was found, so the corner was intentionally torn off. Besides, we here detect the intervention of Father Philibin, for, as you have told me, your assistant Mignot remembers that at his first glance the copy-slip appeared to him to be intact, and that he felt surprised when, after losing sight of it for a moment, he saw it still in Father Philibin's hands and mutilated. So there is no doubt on the point; the corner was torn away by Father Philibin. Throughout the campaign it was he, always he who turned up at decisive moments to save the culprit! And this is why I should like to have complete proof—that is to say, the little fragment of paper which he carried away with him.'

At this David in his turn expressed his surprise: 'You think that he kept it?'

'Certainly I think so. At all events he may have kept it. Philibin is a taciturn man, extremely dexterous, however coarse and heavy he may look. He must have preserved that fragment as a weapon for his own defence, as a means of keeping a hold over his accomplices. I nowadays suspect that, influenced by some motive which remains obscure, he was the great artisan of the iniquity. Perhaps he was merely guided by a spirit of fidelity towards his chief, Father Crabot; perhaps there has been some skeleton between them since that suspicious affair of the donation of Valmarie; perhaps too Philibin was actuated simply by militant faith and a desire to promote the triumph of the Church. At all events he's a terrible fellow, a man of determination and action, by the side of whom that noisy, empty Brother Fulgence is merely a vain fool.'

Marc had begun to ponder. 'Father Philibin, Father Philibin.... Yes, I was altogether mistaken about him. Even after the trial I still thought him a worthy man, a man of upright nature, even if warped by his surroundings.... Yes, yes, he was the great culprit, the artisan of forgery and falsehood.'

But David again turned to Delbos: 'Suppose,' said he, 'that Philibin should have kept the corner which he tore from the slip, you surely don't expect that he will give it to you, if you ask him for it—do you?'

'Oh! no,' the advocate answered with a laugh. 'But before attempting anything decisive I should like to reflect, and ascertain if there is no means of securing the irrefutable proof. Moreover, a demand for the revision of a case is a very serious matter, and nothing ought to be left to chance.... Let me complete our case if I can; give me a few days—two or three weeks if necessary—and then we will act.'

On the morrow Marc understood by his wife's manner that her grandmother had spoken out and that the Congregations, from Father Crabot to the humblest of the Ignorantines, were duly warned. The affair suddenly burst into life again, there came increasing agitation and alarm. Informed as they were of the discovery of the duplicate copy-slip, conscious that the innocent man's family were now on the road to the truth, hourly expecting to see Brother Gorgias denounced, the guilty ones, Brother Fulgence, Father Philibin, and Father Crabot, returned to the fray, striving to hide their former crime by committing fresh ones. They divined that the masterpiece of iniquity which they had reared so laboriously, and defended so fiercely, was now in great peril, and, yielding to that fatality whereby one lie inevitably leads to endless others, they were ready for the worst deeds in order to save their work from destruction. Besides, it was no mere question of protecting themselves, the salvation of the Church would depend on the battle. If the infamous structure of falsehood should collapse, would not the Congregations be buried beneath it? The Brothers' school would be ruined, closed, while the secular school triumphed; the Capuchins' business would be seriously damaged, customers would desert them, their shrine of St. Antony of Padua would be reduced to paltry profits; the college of Valmarie likewise would be threatened, the Jesuits would be forced to quit the region which they now educated under various disguises; and all religious influence would decline, the breach in the flanks of the Church would be enlarged, and free thought would clear the highway to the future. How desperate therefore was the resistance, how fiercely did the whole clerical army arise in order that it might not be compelled to cede aught of the wretched region of error and dolour, which, for ages, it had steeped in night!

Before Brother Gorgias was even denounced, his superiors felt it necessary to defend him, to cover him at all costs, to forestall the threatened attack, by concocting a story which might prove his innocence. At the first moment, however, there was terrible confusion; the Brother was seen hurrying wildly, on his long thin legs, along the streets of Maillebois and the roads of the neighbourhood. With his eagle beak set between his projecting cheek-bones, his deep black eyes, with their thick brows, and his grimacing mouth, he resembled a fierce, scoffing bird of prey. In the course of one day he was seen on the road to Valmarie, then quitting the residence of Philis, the Mayor of Maillebois, then alighting from a train which had brought him from Beaumont. Moreover, both in the town and the surrounding country many cassocks and frocks were encountered hurrying hither and thither, thus testifying to a perfect panic. It was only on the morrow that the meaning of the agitation was made evident by an article in *Le Petit Beaumontais*, announcing in violent language that the whole Simon affair was to be revived by the friends of the ignoble Jew, who were about to agitate the region by denouncing a worthy member of one of the religious Orders, the holiest of men.

Brother Gorgias was not yet named, but from that moment a fresh article appeared every day, and by degrees the version of the affair which the Brother's superiors had concocted was set out in opposition to the version which, it was foreseen, would be given by David, though the latter had revealed it to nobody. However, the desire of the clericals was to wreck it beforehand. Everything was flatly denied. It was impossible that Brother Gorgias could have paused before Zéphirin's window on the night of the crime, for witnesses had proved that he had already returned to the school at half-past ten o'clock. Besides, the initialling on the copy-slip was not his, for the experts had fully recognised Simon's handwriting. And everything could be easily explained. Simon, having procured a writing slip, had imitated the Brother's paraph, which he had found in one of Zéphirin's copybooks. Then, as he knew that the slips were stamped at the Brothers' school, he had torn off one corner with diabolical cunning, in order to create a belief in some precaution taken by the murderer; his infernal object being to cast the responsibility of his own crime on some servant of God, and thereby gratify the hatred of the Church which possessed him—-Jew that he was, fated to everlasting damnation. And this extravagant story, repeated every day, soon became the *credo* of the readers whom the newspaper debased and poisoned with its falsehoods.

It should be mentioned, however, that at the first moment there was a little uncertainty and hesitation, for other explanations had been circulated, and Brother Gorgias himself appeared to have made some curious statements. Formerly hidden away in the background, now suddenly thrust into full light, this Brother Gorgias was an extraordinary character. The Countess de Quédeville, the former owner of Valmarie, had endeavoured to transform his father, Jean Plumet, a poacher, into a kind of gamekeeper. He, the son, had never known his mother, a hussy who rambled about the woods, for she had disappeared soon after his birth. Then his father had been shot one night by an old fellow poacher, and the boy, at that time twelve years old, had remained at Valmarie, protected by the Countess, and becoming the playfellow of her grandson Gaston, with the exact circumstances of whose death, while walking out with Father Philibin, he was doubtless well acquainted, as well as with all that had ensued when the last of the Quédevilles died and bequeathed the estate to Father Crabot. The two Jesuits had never ceased to take an interest in him, and it was thanks to them that he had become an Ignorantine, in spite, it was said, of serious circumstances which tended to prevent it. For these reasons certain evil-minded folk suspected the existence of some corpse between the two Jesuit fathers and their compromising inferior.

At the same time Brother Gorgias was cited as an admirable member of his cloth, one truly imbued with the Holy Spirit. He possessed faith, that sombre, savage faith which pictures man as a weakling, a prey to perpetual sin, ruled by an absolute master, a Deity of wrath and punishment. That Deity alone reigned; it was for the Church to visit His wrath upon the masses, whose duty it became to bow their heads in servile submission until the day of resurrection dawned amid the delights of the heavenly kingdom. He, Brother Gorgias, often sinned himself, but he invariably confessed his transgression with a vehement show of repentance, striking his breast with both fists, and humbling himself in the mud. Then he rose again, absolved, at rest, displaying the provoking serenity of a pure conscience. He had paid his debt, and he would owe nothing more until the weakness of his flesh should cast him into sin again. As a lad he had roamed the woods, growing up amid poaching and thieving, and hiding himself away with the little hussies of the district. Later, after joining the Ignorantines, he had displayed the keenest appetites, showing himself a big eater, a hard drinker, with inclinations towards lubricity and violence. But, as he said in that strangely-compounded, humble, scoffing, threatening way of his to Fathers Philibin and Crabot, whenever they reproached him for some too serious prank: did not everybody sin? did not everybody need forgiveness? Half amusing, half alarming them, he won their pardon, so sincere and stupendous did his remorse appear—remorse which sometimes impelled him to fast for a week at a stretch, and to wear hair-cloths, studded with small sharp nails, next to his skin. It was indeed on this account that he had been always well noted by his superiors, who recognised that he possessed the genuine religious spirit—the spirit which, when his monkish vices ran riot, atoned for them with the avenging flagellation of penitence.

Now, on the revival of the Simon case, Brother Gorgias made the mistake of saying too much in the course of his first confidential chats with the writers of *Le Petit Beaumontais*. No doubt his superiors had not yet expressly imposed their own version on him, and he was too intelligent to be blind to its exceeding absurdity. As another copy of the writing slip, one bearing his paraph, had been discovered, it must have seemed to him ridiculous to deny that this paraph was his writing. All the experts in the world would never prevent full light from being thrown on that point. Thus he gave some inkling of a version of his own, one which was more reasonable than that of his superiors, and in which a part of the truth appeared. For instance, he allowed it to be supposed that he had indeed halted for a moment outside Zéphirin's open window on the night of the crime, that he had engaged in a friendly chat with the little hunchback, and that he had scolded him on seeing on his table a copy-slip which he had taken from the school without permission. Next, however, had come falsehood. He, Gorgias, had gone off, the child had closed his window, then Simon must have come and have committed the horrid crime, Satan suddenly inspiring him to make use of the copy-slip, after which he had opened the window afresh, in order to let it appear that the murderer had fled that way.

But, although this version of the affair was at the first moment given by the newspaper, which declared that it emanated from a most reliable source, it was on the morrow contradicted energetically, even by Brother Gorgias himself, who repaired expressly to the newspaper office to enter his protest. He then swore on the gospel that he had gone straight home on the evening of the crime, and that the initialling on the copy-slip was a forgery in Simon's handwriting, even as the experts had demonstrated. As a matter of fact he was compelled to accept the concoction of his superiors in order that he might be backed up and saved by them. He grumbled over it, and shrugged his shoulders impatiently, for it seemed to him an extremely stupid version; but at the same time he bowed to the decision of the others, even though he foresaw that their system of defence must eventually crumble to pieces.

At this moment Brother Gorgias, with his scoffing impudence and his heroic mendacity, was really superb. But, then, was not the Deity behind him? Was he not lying in order to save Holy Church, knowing too that absolution would wash away his sin? He even dreamt of the palms of martyrdom; each pious act of infamy that he perpetrated would entitle him to another joy in heaven! From that moment, then, he became merely a docile instrument in the hands of Brother Fulgence, behind whom Father Philibin was secretly acting under the discreet orders of Father Crabot. Their tactics were to deny everything, even what was self-evident, for fear lest the smallest breach in the sacred wall of the Congregations should prove the beginning of inevitable ruin; and although their absurd version of the affair might seem idiotic to people possessed of logical minds, it would none the less long remain the only truth accepted by the mass of the faithful, with whom they could presume to do anything, knowing as they did their boundless, fathomless credulity.

The clericals, then, having assumed the offensive without waiting for Gorgias to be denounced, Brother Fulgence in particular displayed the most intemperate zeal. At times of great emotion, his father, the mad doctor who had died in an asylum, seemed to revive in him. With his brain all fogged, unhinged by vanity and ambition, he yielded to the first impulse that came to him, ever dreaming of doing some mighty service to the Church, which would raise him to the head of his Order. Thus, in the earlier stages of the Simon affair, he had lost the little common-sense which he had previously shown, for he had hoped that the case would yield him the glory he coveted; and now that it was revived he once more became delirious. He was constantly to be seen hurrying along the streets of Maillebois, little, dark, and lean, with the folds of his gown flying about him as if a gale were carrying him away. Whenever he entered into conversation he defended his school with passionate eagerness, calling on heaven to witness the angelic purity of his assistants. As for the abominable rumours which had been circulated long ago respecting some Brothers who had been so horribly compromised that it had been necessary to conjure them away with the greatest speed—all those infamous tales were inventions of the devil.

In this respect, perhaps, however contrary to the truth his vehement declarations might be, Brother Fulgence, in the first instance, made them in all good faith, for he lived very much in another world, far from mere reason. But he soon found himself caught beneath the millstone of falsehood; it became necessary that he should lie knowingly and deliberately, and he did so at last with a kind of devout rage, for the very love of God. Was he not, himself, chaste? Had he not always wrestled against temptation? That was so; and he therefore made it his duty to guarantee the absolute chastity of his entire Order; he answered for the Brothers who stumbled by the way, he denied to laymen the right of judging them, for the laymen belonged merely to the flock, they knew nought of the temple. If, then, Brother Gorgias had sinned, he owed account of it to God only, not to man. As a member of a religious Order he had ceased to be liable to human justice. In this way, consumed by his craving to thrust himself forward, Brother Fulgence went on and on, impelled by skilful and discreet hands which piled all responsibilities upon his shoulders.

It was not difficult to divine that Father Philibin stood behind him in the gloom—Father Philibin, who, in his turn, was the instrument of Father Crabot. But how supple and how powerful a one, retaining his personality even amidst his obedience! He willingly exaggerated the characteristics of his peasant origin, affecting the heavy *bon-homie* of some rough-hewed son of the soil; yet he was full of the shrewdest craft, endowed with the patience needed for long enterprises, which he conducted with wonderful dexterity. He was always striving to attain some mysterious object, but he made no stir, he showed no personal ambition; the only joy he coveted was that of seeing his work prosper. Supposing him to be possessed of faith, it must have been a desire to serve his superiors and the Church that impelled him to fight on like an unknown unscrupulous soldier. As Prefect of the Studies at Valmarie he there kept a watch over everything, busied himself with everything; for, however massive his build, he was very active. Mingling with the pupils of the college, playing with them, watching them, studying them, diving to the very depths of their souls, ascertaining everything he could about their relatives and their friends, he possessed the master's all-seeing eye, the mind which stripped the brains and hearts of others.

At times, it was said, he shut himself up with Father Crabot, the Rector, who affected to direct the establishment from on high, never attending personally to the education of the boys; and to him Father Philibin communicated his notes, his reports, his many documents containing the most complete and secret particulars about each pupil. It was asserted that Father Crabot, who prudently made it a principle to keep no papers whatever, did not approve of Philibin's practice of collecting and cataloguing documents. Yet, in recognition of his great services, he let him do so, regarding himself meantime as the directing hand, the superior mind which made use of the other. Indeed, did he not reign from his austere little cell over all the fine folk of the department? Did not the ladies whom he confessed, the families whose children were educated at Valmarie, belong to him by virtue of the might of his sacred ministry? He flattered himself that it was he who wove and disposed the huge net in which he hoped to capture one and all, when in reality it was more frequently Father Philibin who covertly prepared the various campaigns and ensured victory. In the Simon case, in particular, the latter seemed to have been the hidden artisan who recoiled from no task, however dark and base it might be, the politic man whom nothing could disgust, who had remained the friend of that vicious but well-informed youth, Georges Plumet,—nowadays the terrible Brother Gorgias,—following him through life, protecting him because he was as dangerous as useful, and doing all that could be done to extricate him from that frightful affair, the murder of little Zéphirin, in order no doubt that he, Philibin himself, might not come to grief in it, in the company of his superior, Father Crabot, that glory of the Church.

Now, once again, Maillebois became impassioned, though as yet there were only rumours of the criminal devices which the Jews were preparing in order to set the devoted Brother Gorgias, that holy man, revered by the entire district, in the place of that infamous scoundrel Simon. Extraordinary efforts were made to induce the school children's parents—even those whose children attended the secular school—to condemn the revival of the affair. People talked as if the streets had been mined by some hidden band of scoundrels, the enemies of God and France, who had resolved to blow up the town as soon as a certain signal should reach them from abroad. At a sitting of the Municipal Council, Mayor Philis ventured to allude to a vague danger threatening the locality, and denounced the Jews who were secretly piling up millions for the diabolical work. Then, becoming more precise, he condemned the impious doings of the schoolmaster, that Marc Froment, of whom he had hitherto failed to rid the town. But he was still watching him, and this time he hoped that he would compel the Academy Inspector to show exemplary severity.

The successive versions which *Le Petit Beaumontais* had given of Marc's share in the revival of the affair had cast confusion into the minds of many folk. There was certainly a question of a document found at the house of Mesdames Milhomme, the stationers; but some people spoke also of another abominable forgery perpetrated by Simon, and others of a crushing document which proved the complicity of Father Crabot. The only certain thing was that General Jarousse had paid another visit to his cousin, Madame Edouard, that poor relation whose existence he so willingly forgot. One morning he had been seen arriving and rushing into the little shop, whence he had emerged half an hour later, looking extremely red. And the result of his tempestuous intervention was that Madame Alexandre, and her son Sébastien, now convalescent, started on the morrow for the South of France, while Madame Edouard continued to manage the shop to the complete satisfaction of the clerical customers. She ascribed the absence of her sister-in-law to the latter's maternal anxiety, for only a sojourn in a warm climate would restore Sébastien to health; but as a matter of fact she was quite ready to recall Madame Alexandre in the interests of their business, should the secular school prove victorious in the coming contest.

Amid the rumbling of the great storm which was rising, Marc endeavoured to discharge his duties as schoolmaster with all correctitude. The affair was now in David's hands, and in that respect he, Marc, merely had to wait until he could assist him with his evidence. Thus never had he devoted himself more entirely to his pupils, striving to inspire them with reason and kindliness, for his active share in the reparation of one of the most monstrous iniquities of the age had filled him with greater fervour than ever for the cause of human solidarity. With Geneviève he showed himself very affectionate, endeavouring to avoid all subjects on which they disagreed, attentive only, it seemed, to those little trifles which are yet of great importance in one's daily life. But whenever his wife returned from a visit to her relations he divined that she was nervous, impatient, more and more exasperated with him, her mind being full of stories which she had heard from his enemies. Thus he could not always avoid quarrels, which gradually became more and more venomous and deadly.

One evening hostilities broke out on the subject of that unhappy man Férou. Tragic tidings had reached Marc during the day: a sergeant, to whom Férou had behaved rebelliously, had shot him dead with a revolver. Marc, on going to see the widow, had found her in her wretched home, weeping and begging death to take her also, together with her younger daughters, even as it had compassionately taken the eldest one already. Marc felt that Férou's frightful fate was the logical *dénouement* of his career: the poor schoolmaster, scorned, embittered to the point of rebellion, driven from his post, deserting in order that he might not have to pay to the barracks the debt which he had already paid in part to the school, then conquered by hunger, forcibly incorporated in the army when he returned to succour his despairing wife and children, and ending like a mad dog, yonder, under the flaming sky, amid the torturing life of a disciplinary company. At the same time, in presence of the sobbing wife and her stupefied daughters, in presence of those poor ragged waifs whom the iniquity of the social system cast into the last agony, Marc's brotherly and humane nature was stirred to furious protest. Even in the evening he had not calmed down, and forgot himself so far as to speak of the affair to Geneviève, while she was still moving about their bedroom before withdrawing to a small adjoining chamber, where, of recent times, she had slept by herself.

'Do you know the news?' said he. 'A sergeant has blown poor Férou's brains out, in some mutiny, in Algeria.'

'Ah!'

'Yes, I saw Madame Férou this afternoon; she is quite out of her mind.... It was really deliberate, premeditated murder. I don't know if General Jarousse, who showed himself so harsh in Férou's case, will sleep at ease to-night. In any case some of the blood of that poor madman, who was turned into a wild beast, will cling to his hands.'

'It would be very foolish of the general not to sleep!' Geneviève quickly retorted, interpreting Marc's words as an attack on her principles.

He made a gesture of mingled sorrow and indignation. But, recollecting the position, he regretted that he had named the general, for the latter was one of Father Crabot's dearest penitents, and at one moment there had been some thought of using him for a military *coup d'état*. A Bonapartist by repute, with a decorative, corpulent figure, he was very severe with his men, though jovial at bottom, and fond of the table and wenches. Of course there was no harm in that; but, after some negotiations, the clericals found that he was decidedly too big a fool for their purpose; and so he remained a mere possible makeshift for their party, though they still treated him with some consideration.

'When we first knew the Férou family at Le Moreux,' Marc gently resumed, 'they were already so poor, so burdened with work and worries in their wretched school, that I cannot think of that unhappy man, that master, tracked and destroyed like a wolf, without a feeling of anguish and compassion.'

At this Geneviève, thoroughly upset, her earlier displeasure turning into a kind of nervous exasperation, burst into tears. 'Yes, yes! I understand you perfectly—I am a heartless creature, eh? You began by thinking me a fool, and now you believe I have an evil heart. How is it possible for us to continue loving one another if you treat me as though I were a stupid and malicious woman?'

Astonished and grieved at having provoked such an outburst Marc wished to pacify his wife. But she became quite wild. 'No, no! it is all over between us. As you hate me more and more each day, it is best that we should separate at once, without waiting till unworthy things happen!'

Then she rushed into the little room where she now slept, and locked the door with no gentle hand. He, when he saw it thus shut upon him, remained in despair, with tears welling to his eyes. Hitherto that door had always been left open, and, though the husband and wife had no longer shared the same bed, they had remained in a degree together, able to converse with one another. But now came total separation: henceforth they would live as strangers.

On the following evenings Geneviève in the same manner locked herself in her room. Then, having acquired that habit, she never showed herself to Marc until she was fully dressed. As the time approached for the birth of the child she expected, she displayed increasing repugnance for the slightest caress, the merest touch, even, on the part of her husband. He had ascribed this at first to her state of health; but he became surprised as her repulsion developed more and more into hatred, for it seemed to him that the advent of another child ought to have drawn them more closely together. And his anxiety augmented; for if, on the one hand, he was aware that as long as man and woman are united by love no rupture is possible, for the bitterest quarrels evaporate amid their kisses, on the other he knew that, as soon as virtual divorce is agreed upon, the slightest conflict may prove deadly, beyond possibility of reconciliation; indeed, it often happens when homes are seen collapsing in a seemingly inexplicable manner, that everything can be traced back to the severance of the carnal bond, the tie of passion. As long as Geneviève had hung about his neck Marc had not feared the attempts which were made to take her from him. He knew that she was his, he knew that no power in the world could conquer love. But if she ceased to regard him with love and passion, would not the fierce efforts of his enemies at last wrest her from him? And, as day by day he saw her become colder and colder, his heart was wrung by increasing, intolerable anxiety.

At one moment some little enlightenment came to him with respect to the change in his wife's manner. He learnt that she had quitted Abbé Quandieu to take as her confessor Father Théodose, the Superior of the Capuchins, who stage-managed so cleverly the miracles of St. Antony of Padua. The reason given for this change was the discomfort, the unappeased hungry state in which she was left by the ministrations of the priest of St. Martin's. He was now too lukewarm for her ardent faith; whereas handsome Father Théodose, whose fervour was so lofty, would nourish her with the wholemeal bread of mysticism, which she needed to satisfy her. In reality, it was Father Crabot, now sovereign lord at Madame Duparque's house, who had decided on this change, doubtless in order to hasten victory after proceeding with such artful slowness.

It never occurred to Marc to suspect Geneviève of any base intrigue with the Capuchin, that superbly-built man, Christlike in features but of dark complexion, whose large glowing eyes and frizzy beard sent his penitents into raptures. Marc knew his wife to be possessed of too much loyalty and too much dignity, both of mind and body—a dignity that had never forsaken her even in moments of the most passionate rapture. But without carrying matters as far as that, was it not admissible that the growing influence of Father Théodose was in part the domination of a handsome man over a woman who was still young—a man, too, godlike in appearance, and godlike claiming obedience? After her pious conversations with Father Théodose, after the long hours she spent in the confessional, Geneviève returned to her husband quivering, distracted, such as he had never seen her when she retuned from her visits to Abbé Quandieu. In her intercourse with her new confessor she was certainly forming some mystical passion, finding some new food for her craving nature. Perhaps, too, the monk availed himself of her perturbed state of health to terrorise her. Indeed, was not the father of the child she bore one of the damned? She repeatedly spoke of that child in a despairing way, as if seized with a kind of terror, like one of those mothers who dread lest they should give birth to a monster. And if that happily should not come to pass, how would she protect the child from surrounding sin, whither might she carry her babe to save it from the contamination of its father's sacrilegious home? All this threw a little light on Geneviève's rupture with Marc—a rupture in which there might well be remorse at the thought that her child was also the child of an unbeliever; then a vow that she would never more be the mother of that unbeliever's children; and, finally, a perversion and exasperation of love, which dreamt of finding satisfaction henceforth in the *au-delà* of desire. Yet how much still remained obscure, and how cruelly did Marc suffer as he saw himself forsaken by that adored wife, whom the Church was wrenching from his arms, in order that by torturing him it might annihilate him and his work of human liberation!

One day, on returning home after one of her long conferences with Father Théodose, Geneviève, who looked both excited and exhausted, said to Louise, who at that moment came in from school: 'To-morrow at five o'clock you will have to go to confession at the Capuchins'. If you do not confess, you will no longer be received at the Catechism class.'

But Marc resolutely intervened. While allowing Louise to follow the Catechism class, he had hitherto strongly opposed her attendance at confession. 'Louise will not go to the Capuchins',' he said, firmly. 'You know, my dear, that I have given way on every other point, but I will not allow the child to go to confession.'

'Why not?' exclaimed Geneviève, still restraining herself.

'I cannot repeat my reasons before the child. But you know them, and I will not allow my daughter's mind to be soiled, under the pretext of absolving her of trivial faults, which her parents alone need know and correct.'

An explanation, indeed, had taken place between Marc and Geneviève on this subject. In his opinion it was most loathsome and abominable that a little girl should be initiated to the passions of the flesh by a man who, by his very vow of chastity, might be led to every curiosity and every sexual aberration. For ten priests who might be prudent, it was sufficient there should be one of unbalanced mind, and then confession became filth, to which risk Marc refused to expose his daughter Louise. Besides, in that disturbing promiscuity, that secret colloquy amid the mystical, enervating atmosphere and gloom of a chapel, there was not merely the possibility of demoralisation for a girl only twelve years old,—an anxious age, when the senses begin to quicken,—there was also a seizure of her mind and person; for whatever she might become later, girl, wife, and mother, she would always remain the initiate of that minister, who by his very questions had violated her modesty, and thereby affianced her to his jealous Deity. From that time forward, indeed, woman, by her avowals, belonged to her confessor, became his trembling, obedient thing, ever ready to do his behests, to serve, in his hands, as an instrument of investigation and enthralment.

'If our daughter should be guilty of any fault,' Marc resumed, 'she shall confess it to you or me, whenever she feels a need to do so. That will be more logical and cleaner.'

Geneviève shrugged her shoulders, like one who deemed that solution to be both blasphemous and grotesque. 'I won't discuss the matter any further with you,' she said. 'But just tell me this—if you prevent Louise from going to confession, how will she be able to go to her first Communion?'

'Her first Communion? But is it not settled that she will wait till her twentieth birthday in order to decide that question herself? I have let her go to the Catechism class, even as she goes to her *cours* of history and sciences—that is, in order that she may form an opinion and decide later on.'

At this Geneviève's anger mastered her. She turned towards her daughter: 'And you, Louise, what do you think; what do you desire?'

The child, whose usually gay face had become quite grave, had listened to her father and mother in silence. Whenever such quarrels arose, she endeavoured to remain neutral from a fear of embittering matters. Her intelligent eyes glanced from one to the other of her parents as if begging that they would not make themselves unhappy on her account, for she was grieved indeed to find that she was so constantly the cause of their disputes. But, though she showed great deference and affection for her mother, the latter felt that she inclined towards her father, whom indeed she worshipped, and whose firm sense and passion for truth and equity she had inherited.

For a moment Louise remained as if undecided, looking at her parents in her usual affectionate way. Then she gently said: 'What I think, what I wish, mamma? Why, I should much like it to be whatever you and papa might agree upon. But does papa's desire seem to you so very unreasonable? Why not wait a little?'

The mother, quite beside herself, refused to listen any further. 'That is not an answer, my girl,' she cried. 'Remain with your father since you can no longer show me either respect or obedience! You will end, between you, by driving me from the house!'

Then she rushed away and shut herself up in her little room, as she always did nowadays whenever she encountered the slightest opposition. This was her method of ending their quarrels, and on each occasion she seemed to draw farther and farther away from her husband and her child, to set more and more space between herself and the dearly-loved family fireside of other days.

Her belief that attempts were being made to influence her daughter in order that the child might cast off her authority was strengthened by a fresh incident. After long and skilful manœuvring, Mademoiselle Rouzaire had at last secured the post of first assistant teacher at Beaumont, which post she had coveted for years. Inspector Le Barazer had yielded in the matter to the pressing applications of the clerical deputies and senators, at the head of whom Count Hector de Sanglebœuf marched with the noisy bustling gait of a great captain. But to compensate politically for this step, Le Barazer, with his usual maliciousness, had caused the vacant post at Maillebois to be assigned to Mademoiselle Mazeline, the schoolmistress at Jonville, whose good sense Marc so greatly admired. Perhaps, also, the Academy Inspector, who still covertly supported Marc, had desired to place a friend beside him, one whose object would be the same as his own, who would not try to thwart him at every step, as Mademoiselle Rouzaire had done. At all events, when Mayor Philis, in the name of the Municipal Council, complained to Le Barazer of this appointment, which, said he, would place the little girls of Maillebois in the hands of an unbelieving woman, the Academy Inspector affected great astonishment. What! had he not acted in accordance with Count Hector de Sanglebœuf's pressing application? Was it his fault if, owing to promotions among the school staff, a most meritorious person, of whom no parents had ever complained, had become entitled in due order to the post at Maillebois?

As a matter of fact, Mademoiselle Mazeline's *début* in the town proved very successful. People were struck by her gay serenity, the maternal manner in which from the very first day she gained the affection of her pupils. All gentleness and zeal, she directed her efforts in such wise that her daughters, as she called them, might become worthy women, wives, and mothers. But she did not take them to Mass, and she suppressed processions, prayers, and Catechism lessons. Before long, therefore, a few other mothers, who belonged to the clerical faction, like Geneviève, began to protest. Indeed, though she had no cause to congratulate herself on her intercourse with Mademoiselle Rouzaire, whose intrigues had disturbed her home, she now seemed to regret her, and spoke of the new schoolmistress as a most suspicious character, who was capable of the blackest enterprises.

'You hear me, Louise,' she said one day; 'if Mademoiselle Mazeline should say anything wrong to you, you must tell me. I won't allow my daughter's soul to be stolen from me!'

Marc could not refrain from intervening. 'Mademoiselle Mazeline stealing souls!' said he; 'that's foolish! When we were at Jonville you used to admire her, as I did. No woman has a loftier mind or a more tender heart.'

'Oh! naturally you back her up,' Geneviève replied; 'you are well fitted to understand each other. Go and join her, hand our daughter over to her, since I am no longer of any account!'

Then, once again, Geneviève hastened to her room, where little Louise had to join her, weep with her, and entreat her for hours before she could be induced to attend to the home again.

All at once some almost incredible news reached Maillebois, throwing the town into no little emotion. Advocate Delbos, who had gone to Paris and addressed himself to some of the Government departments, laying before the officials the famous duplicate copy-slip furnished by Madame Alexandre, had prevailed on them—by what high influence nobody knew—to order a perquisition in Father Philibin's rooms at Valmarie. The extraordinary part of the affair was the lightning-like speed with which this perquisition was made, the Commissary of Police arriving at the College quite unexpectedly, then at once examining the collection of documents formed by the Prefect of the Studies, and, in the second portfolio he opened, discovering an envelope, already yellow with age, which contained the fragment of the copy-slip torn off so long ago. There was no question of denying its authenticity, for when placed in position at the corner of the mutilated slip it fitted exactly.

It was added that Father Philibin, whom Father Crabot—utterly upset by the affair—immediately interrogated, had made a frank confession, explaining his conduct by a kind of instinctive impulse, his hand having acted before his mind had time to think, so great had been his anxiety on seeing the stamp of the Brother's school upon the copy-slip, when he found the latter in Zéphirin's room. If he had remained silent afterwards, this was because a careful study of the affair had convinced him that Simon was indeed the culprit, and had intentionally made use of what was evidently a gross forgery in order to injure religion. Thus Father Philibin gloried in his act, for by tearing off that corner and afterwards preserving silence, he had behaved like a hero who set Holy Church high above the justice of men. Would not a vulgar accomplice have destroyed the fragment? As the reverend Father had preserved it, could one not understand that it had been his intention to re-establish all the facts whenever it might become advisable to do so? Such was the language held by some of his partisans, but there were folk who attributed the preservation of the fragment to his mania for keeping even the smallest scraps of paper, and who thought also that he had wished to remain in possession of a weapon which might prove useful against others.

It was said that Father Crabot, who for his part destroyed even the cards which visitors left for him, was exasperated with his colleague, and that in his surprise and fury at the first moment he had cried: 'What! I gave him orders to burn everything, and he kept that!' In any case, on the evening of the day when the discovery was made by the Commissary, Father Philibin, against whom as yet no warrant had been issued, disappeared. When pious souls anxiously inquired what had become of him, they were told that Father Poirier, the Provincial of Beaumont, had decided to send him to a convent in Italy to observe a retreat; and there, as if engulfed, he was at once buried in eternal silence.

The revision of Simon's case now appeared to be inevitable. Delbos sent for David and Marc, in order to decide in what form the necessary application to the Minister of Justice should be made. The discovery of the long-missing corner of the copy-slip would alone suffice for the sentence of the Court of Beaumont to be quashed, and the advocate was of opinion that they ought to content themselves with this discovery, and, for the time at all events, leave on one side the illegal communication which Judge Gragnon had made to the jurors. Moreover, the circumstances of that communication, now difficult of proof, would be brought to light during the new investigations which must ensue. Meantime, as the truth in the matter of the copy-slip was manifest, as the report of the handwriting experts was entirely upset, the origin of the stamped and initialled slip constituting such a damaging element in the case that Father Philibin had practised dissimulation and falsehood to conceal it, the advocate considered it best to assail Brother Gorgias without more ado. When Marc and David quitted Delbos that decision had been adopted; and on the morrow David addressed to the Minister a letter in which he formally accused Brother Gorgias of having committed a heinous offence on little Zéphirin, and murdered him, for which crimes his, David's, brother Simon had been in penal servitude for ten years.

Emotion then reached a climax. On the day after the discovery of the corner of the copy-slip among Father Philibin's papers, there had come an hour of lassitude and discomfiture among the most ardent supporters of the Church. This time the battle really seemed to be lost, and *Le Petit Beaumontais* even printed an article in which the conduct of the reverend Jesuit was roundly blamed. But two days later the faction had recovered its self-possession, and the very same newspaper proceeded to canonise theft and falsehood. St. Philibin, hero and martyr, was portrayed amid a setting of palms, and with a halo about his head. A legend likewise arose, showing the reverend Father in a remote convent of the Apennines, surrounded by wild forests. There, wearing a hair-cloth next his skin, he prayed devoutly both by day and by night, and offered himself in sacrifice for the sins of the world. And on the back of the pious little pictures which circulated, showing him on his knees, there was a prayer by repeating which the faithful might gain indulgences.

The resounding accusation launched against Brother Gorgias fully restored to the clericals their rageful determination to attack and conquer, convinced as they were that the victory of the Jew would shake the Congregations in a terrible fashion and leave a gaping breach in the very heart of the Church. All the anti-Simonists of former days rose up again, more uncompromising than ever, eager to conquer or to die. And the old battle began afresh on every side; on one hand all the free-minded men who believed in truth and equity and looked to the future, on the other all the reactionaries, the believers in authority, who clung to the past with its God of wrath, and based salvation on priests and soldiers. The Municipal Council of Maillebois again quarrelled about schoolmaster Froment, families were rent asunder, the Brothers' pupils and Marc's stoned one another on the Place de la République after lessons. Then, too, the fine society of Beaumont was utterly upset, such was the feverish anxiety of all who had participated in any way in Simon's trial.

For one man, such as Salvan, who rejoiced with Marc at each successive interview, how many there were who no longer slept o' nights at the thought that all the iniquity which had been buried was about to be exhumed! Fresh elections were impending, and the politicians feared lest they should be unseated. Lemarrois, the Radical, the ex-Mayor of Beaumont, once the town's indispensable man, was terrified by the rise of Delbos's popularity; Marcilly, the amiable *arriviste*, ever anxious to be on the winning side, floundered in uncertainty, no longer knowing which party to support; the reactionary senators and deputies, headed by the fierce Hector de Sanglebœuf, resisted desperately as they saw the storm, which might sweep them away, rising all round. In the government world and the university world the anxiety was no less keen; Prefect Hennebise lamented that he could not stifle the affair; Rector Forbes, losing his depth, cast everything upon the shoulders of Academy Inspector Le Barazer, who alone remained calm and smiling amid the tempest, while Depinvilliers, the Director of the Lycée, took his daughters to Mass despairingly, even as one may throw oneself into a river, and Inspector Mauraisin, in anguish and astonishment at the turn which things were taking, wondered if the time had not come to go over to the Freemasons. [2]

[2] The French Freemasons are largely identified with Republican and anti-Catholic views.—*Trans.*

But the emotion was particularly keen in the judicial world, for did not a revision of the former trial mean a new trial directed against the judges who had conducted the first proceedings? and if the papers in the case should be exhumed and examined would not terrible revelations ensue? Investigating Magistrate Daix, that unlucky honest man, who was haunted by remorse for having yielded to his wife's covetous ambition, looked livid when he repaired in silence each morning to his office at the Palace of Justice. And if Raoul de La Bissonnière, the dapper Public Prosecutor, made, on the contrary, an excessive show of good humour and ease of mind, one could divine that he did so from a torturing desire to prevent his fears from being seen. As for Presiding Judge Gragnon, who was the most compromised of all, he seemed to have aged quite suddenly; his face had become heavy, his shoulders bent beneath some invisible weight, and he dragged his big body about with shuffling steps, unless he noticed that he was being watched, when, with a suspicious glance, he made an effort to draw himself erect. Meantime the gentlemen's ladies had once more transformed their *salons* into hotbeds of intrigue, barter, and propaganda. And from the *bourgeois* to their servants, from the servants to the tradespeople, from the tradespeople to the working classes, the whole population followed on, becoming more and more crazed amid the tempest which cast men and things into general dementia.

The sudden self-effacement of Father Crabot, whose tall and elegant figure and whose handsome gowns of fine cloth were so well known at the reception hour in the Avenue des Jaffres, was much remarked. He ceased to show himself there, and a proof of excellent taste and profound piety was detected in his desire for retreat and meditation, of which his friends spoke with devout emotion. As Father Philibin also had disappeared, the only one of the superior ecclesiastics who remained in the front rank was Brother

Fulgence, who somehow always contrived to act in a compromising way, bestirring himself too much, showing indeed such clumsiness at each step he took that nasty rumours began to circulate among the clericals, in accordance, no doubt, with some order from Valmarie to sacrifice the Brother.

But the hero, the extraordinary figure of the time, one that became more and more amazing every day, was Brother Gorgias, who met the accusation brought against him with prodigious audacity. On the very evening of the day when David's letter denouncing him was made public, he hastened to the office of *Le Petit Beaumontais* to answer it, insulting the Jews, inventing extraordinary stories, clothing true facts with falsehoods of genius, fit to disturb the soundest minds. He scoffed, too, asking if schoolmasters were in the habit of walking about with copy-slips in their pockets; and he denied everything, both paraph and stamp, explaining that Simon, who had imitated his handwriting, might very well have procured a stamp from the Brothers' school, or even have had one made. It was idiotic; but he nevertheless proclaimed this version in such a thundering voice and with such violent gestures that it was accepted, and became official truth. From that moment *Le Petit Beaumontais* showed no hesitation; it adopted the story of the forged stamp as it had adopted that of the forged paraph, the whole theory of abominable premeditation on the part of Simon, who, in committing his crime, had sought with infernal cunning to cast it upon a holy man, in order to soil the Church! And this imbecile invention impassioned all the folk who were brutified by centuries of Catechism and bondage. Brother Gorgias rose to be a martyr of the Faith, like Father Philibin.

He could no longer show himself without being acclaimed, women kissed the hem of his frock, children asked him to bless them, while he, impudent and triumphant, harangued the crowds, and indulged in the most extravagant mummery, like a popular idol, a mountebank before a booth, certain of applause. Yet, behind all that assurance, those who were warned, who knew the truth, detected the anxious distress of that wretched man who was forced to play a part, the folly and fragility of which he was the first to recognise. And it was evident that in him one simply had an actor on the stage, a tragic puppet whose strings were pulled by invisible hands. Though Father Crabot had hidden himself away, humbly cloistered himself in his bare, cold cell at Valmarie, his black shadow still passed across the scene, and one could divine that his were the dexterous hands which pulled the strings, pushed the puppets forward, and toiled for the triumph of the Congregations.

Amid the greatest commotion, and despite the opposition of all the coalesced reactionary forces, the Minister of Justice was obliged to lay the application for revision, drawn up by David on behalf of Madame Simon and her children, before the Court of Cassation. This was truth's first victory, and for a moment the clerical faction seemed to be overwhelmed. But on the morrow the struggle began afresh. Even the Court of Cassation was cast into the mud, insulted every morning, accused of having sold itself to the Jews. *Le Petit Beaumontais* enumerated the amounts which had been paid, libelled the presiding judge, the general prosecutor, and the counsellors by relating all sorts of abominable stories about their private lives, which stories were inventions from beginning to end. During the two months occupied by the preparation of the case the river of filth never ceased to flow; no manœuvre, however iniquitous, no lie, even no crime, was left untried to stay the march of inexorable justice. At last, after memorable discussions, during which several judges gave a high example of healthy common-sense and courageous equity, superior to all passion, the Court gave its decision, which, although foreseen, burst on its slanderers like a thunderclap. It retained the cause, declared that there was ground for revision, and recognised the necessity of an investigation, which it decided to conduct itself.

That evening Marc, when afternoon lessons were over, found himself alone in his little garden, in the warm twilight of springtime. Louise had not yet come in from school, for Mademoiselle Mazeline, whose favourite pupil she had become, sometimes kept her with her. As for Geneviève, ever since *déjeuner*, she had been absent at her grandmother's, where, indeed, she now spent nearly all her time. And, despite the fresh perfume which the lilacs shed in the warm air, Marc, as he paced the garden paths, was pursued by bitter, torturing thoughts of his devastated home. He had not given way on the subject of Confession—indeed, his daughter had lately quitted the Catechism class, the priest having refused to receive her any longer if she did not come to him by way of the Confessional. But, morning and evening alike, Marc had to contend against the attacks of his wife, who was exasperated, maddened, by the idea that Louise would be damned, and that she herself would be virtually an accomplice in it as she could not find the strength to take the girl in her arms and carry her to the tribunal of penitence. She remembered her own adorable first Communion, the loveliest day of her life, with her white gown, the incense, the candles, the gentle Jesus to whom she had so sweetly affianced herself, and who had remained her only real spouse, the spouse of a divine love, the delights of which—she vowed it—were the only ones which she would taste henceforth. But was her daughter to be robbed of such felicity, degraded, reduced to the level of the beasts of the field, which knew no religion? She could not bear such a thought, but sought every possible opportunity to wring a consent from her husband, changing the family hearth into a battlefield, where the most futile incidents gave rise to endless bickering.

The night was falling, slowly and peacefully; and Marc, on whom for the moment a feeling of great lassitude had come, felt astonished that he should be able to resist his wife with a courage which was cruel for her, himself, and their daughter. All his old spirit of tolerance came back; he had allowed his daughter to be baptised, so might he not also allow her to make her first Communion? The reasons which his wife urged, reasons to which he had long bowed—respect of individual liberty, the rights of a mother, the rights of conscience—were not without weight. In a home the mother necessarily became the educator and initiator, particularly when girls were in question. To take no account of her ideas, to oppose the desires of her mind and heart, meant surely the wrecking of the home. Nought was left of the bond of agreement which a home requires to flourish, all happiness was destroyed, the parents and their child lapsed into horrible warfare—that warfare from which Marc's own home, once so united and so sweet, now suffered. And thus, while pacing the narrow paths of his little garden, across which the shadows were spreading, Marc asked himself whether and in what manner he might give way again in order to restore a little peace and happiness.

A feeling of remorse tortured him; for was not his misfortune due to himself? His share of responsibility had become manifest to him more than once, and he had asked himself why, on the morrow of his marriage, he had not endeavoured to win Geneviève over to his own belief. At that time, amid the first revelation of love, she had indeed belonged to him, she had cast herself into his arms with all confidence, ready to mingle with him, in such wise that they might be of one flesh and one mind. He alone, at that unique hour of life, might have had the power to wrest the woman from the priest, and turn the child of the ages, bending beneath the dread of hell, into the conscious companion of his own existence, a companion whose mind would be freed, opened to truth and equity.

At the time of their earliest quarrels Geneviève herself had cried it to him: 'If you suffer because we do not think the same, it is your own fault! You should have taught me. I am such as I was made, and the misfortune is that you did not know how to make me anew!'

She had got far beyond that point now; she did not allow that he could possibly influence her, such had become the unshakable pride of her faith. Nevertheless, he bitterly recalled his lost opportunity, and deplored his egotistical adoration during the delightful springtime of their married life, when he had never ceased to admire her beauty, without a thought of diving into her conscience and enlightening her. True, he had not then imagined that he would become an artisan of truth such as he was to-day; he had accepted certain compromises, imagining that he was strong enough to remain the master. Indeed, all his present torture arose from his whilom masculine vanity, the blind weakness of his early love.

He knew that now, and as he paused before a lilac bush, whose flowers, open since the previous day, were shedding a penetrating perfume around, a sudden flame, a renewed desire to fight and conquer, arose within him. Even if he had formerly failed in his duty, was that a reason for him to fail in it now, by allowing his daughter to wreck her life in the same way as her mother had wrecked hers? Such remissness on his part would be the more unpardonable as he had taken on himself the task of saving the children of others from the falsehoods of the centuries. Perhaps it might be allowable for some obscurely situated man to put up with the doings of a bigot wife, who was intent on crazing her daughter with foolish and dangerous practices; but how could he accept such a position—he who had removed the crucifix from his classroom, he whose teaching was strictly secular, he who openly proclaimed the necessity of saving woman from the Church if one desired to build the Happy City? Would not his acceptance of such a position be the fullest possible confession of impotence? It would be the denial and the annihilation of his mission. He would lose all power, all authority to ask others to do that which he could or would not do himself in his own home. And what an example of hypocrisy and egotistical weakness would he not give to his daughter, who was acquainted with his ideas, and knew him to be opposed to Confession and Communion. Would she not wonder why he tolerated at home the actions which he condemned when their neighbours were in question? Would it not seem to her that he thought one way and acted another? Ah! no, no, tolerance had become impossible; he could no longer give way unless he desired to see his work of deliverance crumble beneath universal contempt.

Once more Marc began to walk to and fro under the paling sky, where the first stars were beginning to twinkle. One of the triumphs of the Church was that freethinking parents did not remove their children from its control, bound as they were by social usages, and fearful of scandal. There was an apprehension among them that they might fail to start their sons in life, or find husbands for their daughters, if the children did not at least pass through the formal routine of the sacraments. So who would begin, who would set the example? No doubt it would be necessary to wait a very long time for a general change, the time which science might require to destroy dogma as a matter of usage, even as it had already destroyed it as a matter of sense. Yet it was the duty of brave minds to set the first examples, examples which the Church dreaded, and which nowadays impelled it to make so many efforts to retain the support and favour of women, whom it had so long brutalised, treated as daughters of the devil, responsible for all the sins of the world.

It seemed to Marc that the Jesuits, who by a stroke of genius had resolved to adapt the Deity to the requirements of human passions, were the real artisans of the great movement which had placed women as instruments of political and social conquest in the hands of the priests. The Church had cursed human love, and now it employed it. It had treated woman as a monster of lewdness, from whom it was the duty of the Saints to flee; yet now it caressed her, loaded her with flattery, made her the ornament and mainstay of the sanctuary, having resolved to exploit her power over man.

Indeed sexuality flames among the candles of the altars, the priests nowadays accept it as a means of grace, use it as a trap in which they hope to recapture and master man. Does not all the disunion, the painful quarrel of contemporary society, spring from the divorce existing between man and woman, the former half freed, the latter still a serf, a petted, hallucinated slave of expiring Catholicism? The problem lies in that; we men should not leave the Church to profit by the mystical rapture in which it steeps our daughters and our wives, we should wrest from it the merit of the spurious deliverance it brings to them, we should deliver them really from all their fancies, and take them from the Church to ourselves, since indeed they are ours, even as we are theirs.

Marc reflected that there were three forces in presence: man, woman, and the Church, and instead of woman and the Church being arrayed against man, it was necessary that man and woman should be arrayed against the Church. Besides, were not man and wife one? Neither could act without the other, whereas united in flesh and in mind they became invincible, the very force of life, the very embodiment of happiness in the midst of conquered nature. And the one, sole, true solution suddenly became manifest to Marc: woman must be taught, enlightened, she must be set in her rightful place as our equal and our companion, for only the freed woman can free man.

At the moment when, calmed and comforted, Marc was regaining the courage he needed to continue fighting, he heard Geneviève come in, and went to join her in the classroom where a little vague light still lingered. He found her standing there, and though the birth of the child she expected was now near at hand, she carried herself so upright, in such an aggressive posture, with such brilliant eyes, that he felt a supreme storm to be imminent.

'Well, are you pleased?' she asked him curtly.

'Pleased with what, my darling?'

'Ah! you don't know then.... So I shall have the pleasure of being the first to give you the great news.... Your heroic efforts have been successful, the news has just arrived by telegraph. The Court of Cassation has decided in favour of the revision of the affair.'

Marc raised a cry of intense joy, unwilling to notice the tone of furious irony in which Geneviève had announced the triumph: 'At last! So there are some real judges after all! The innocent man will suffer no longer.... But is the news quite certain?'

'Yes, yes, quite certain, I had it from honourable people to whom it was telegraphed. Yes, the abomination is complete and you may well rejoice.'

In Geneviève's quivering bitterness there was an echo of the violent scene which, doubtless, she had just witnessed at her grandmother's house, whither some priest or monk, some friend of Father Crabot's, had hastened to impart the tidings of the catastrophe which imperilled religion.

But Marc, as if determined not to understand, opened his arms to his wife, saying: 'Thank you; I could not have had a better-loved messenger. Kiss me!'

Geneviève brushed him aside with a gesture of hatred. 'Kiss you!' she cried. 'Why? Because you have been the artisan of an infamous deed; because this criminal victory over religion rejoices you? It is your country, your family, yourself, that you cast into the mire in order to save that filthy Jew, the greatest scoundrel in all the world!'

'Do not say such things,' replied Marc in a gentle, entreating way, seeking to pacify her. 'How can you repeat such monstrous words, you who used to be so intelligent and so kind-hearted? Is it true, then, that error is so contagious that it may obscure the soundest minds? Just think a little. You know all; Simon is innocent; and to leave him still in penal servitude would be frightful iniquity—a source of social rottenness which would end by destroying the nation.'

'No, no!' she cried, with a kind of mystical exaltation; 'Simon is guilty—men of recognised holiness accused him, and accuse him still; and to regard him as innocent it would be necessary to discard all faith in religion, to believe God Himself capable of error! No, no! he must stay at the galleys, for on the day of his release nothing divine, nothing that one may revere, would be left on earth!'

Marc was becoming impatient. 'I cannot understand,' said he, 'how we can disagree on so clear a question of truth and justice. Heaven has nothing to do with this.'

'It has. There is no truth or justice outside heaven!'

'Ah! that is the gist of it all—that explains our disagreement and torture! You would still think as I do if you had not set heaven between us! And you will come back to me on the day when you consent to live on earth and show a healthy mind and a sisterly heart. There is only one truth, one justice, such as science establishes under the control of human certainty and solidarity!'

Geneviève was becoming exasperated: 'Let us come to the point once and for all,' she retorted. 'It is my religion that you wish to destroy!'

'Yes,' he cried; 'it is against your Roman Catholicism that I fight—against the imbecility of its teaching, the hypocrisy of its practices, the perversion of its worship, its deadly action on children and women, and its social injuriousness. The Roman Catholic Church—that is the enemy of whom we must first clear the path. Before the social question, before the political question, comes the religious question, which bars everything. We shall never be able to take a single forward step unless we begin by striking down that Church, which corrupts, and poisons, and murders. And, understand me fully, that is the reason why I am resolved not to allow our Louise to confess and communicate. I should feel that I was not doing my duty, that I was placing myself in contradiction with all my principles and lessons, if I were to allow such things. And on the morrow I should have to leave this school and cease to teach the children of others, for lack of having both the loyalty and the strength to guide my own child towards truth, the only real and only good truth. Thus I shall not yield on the matter; our daughter herself will come to a decision when she is twenty!'

Geneviève, now quite beside herself, was on the point of replying, when Louise came in, followed by Mademoiselle Mazeline, who, having detained her after lessons, wished to explain that she had been teaching her a difficult crochet stitch. Short and slight, possessed of no beauty, but extremely charming with her broad face, her large, loving mouth, and her fine black eyes glowing with ardent sympathy, the schoolmistress called from the threshold: 'Why, have you no light? I want to show you the clever work of a good little girl.'

But Geneviève, without listening, sternly called the child to her. 'Ah! so it's you, Louise. Come here a moment. Your father is again torturing me about you. He is now positively opposed to your making your first Communion. Well, I insist on your doing so this year. You are twelve years old, you can delay the matter no longer without causing a scandal. But before deciding on my course, I wish to know what your own views are.'

Tall as she was already, Louise looked almost a little woman, showing a very intelligent face, in which her mother's refined features seemed to mingle in an expression of quiet good sense, which she had inherited from her father. With an air of affectionate deference she answered: 'My views! Oh, mamma, I can have none. Only I thought it was all settled, as papa's only desire is that I should wait till my majority. Then I will tell you my views!'

'Is that how you answer me, unhappy child?' cried her mother, whose irritation was increasing. 'Wait! still wait! when your father's horrible lessons are evidently corrupting you, and robbing me more and more of your heart!'

At this moment Mademoiselle Mazeline made the mistake of intervening, but she did so like a good soul who was grieved by this quarrel in a home whose happiness in former days had greatly touched her. 'Oh, my dear Madame Froment!' she said, 'your Louise is very fond of you, and what she said just now was very reasonable.'

Geneviève turned violently towards the schoolmistress: 'Attend to your own affairs, mademoiselle. I won't inquire into your share in all this; but you would do well to teach your pupils to respect God and their parents!... This is not your home, remember!'

Then, as the schoolmistress withdrew, heavy at heart and saying nothing for fear lest she might embitter the quarrel, the mother again turned to the girl:

'Listen to me, Louise ... and you, Marc, listen to me also.... I have had enough of it, I swear to you that I have had enough of it, that what has occurred this evening, what has just been said, has filled the cup to overflowing.... You no longer have any love for me, you torture me in my faith, and you try to drive me from the house.'

Her daughter, full of distress and agitation, was weeping in a corner of the large, dim room, and the heart of her husband, who stood there motionless, bled as he heard those supreme, rending words. Both he and the child raised the same protest: 'Drive you from the house!'

'Yes, you do all you can to render it unbearable!... Indeed, it is impossible for me to remain longer in a spot where all is scandal, error, and impiety, where every word and every gesture wound and shock me. I have been told twenty times that it was not a fit place for me, and I will not damn myself with you, so I am going away, returning whence I came!'

She cried those last words aloud with extraordinary vehemence.

'To your grandmother's, eh?' exclaimed Marc.

'To my grandmother's, yes! That is an asylum, a refuge full of sovereign peace. They at least know how to understand and love me there! I ought never to have quitted that pious home of my youth. Good-bye! There is nothing here to detain either my body or my soul!'

She went towards the door, with a fierce, set face, but, owing to her condition, with somewhat unsteady steps. Louise was still sobbing violently. But Marc, making a last effort, resolutely strove to bar the way.

'In my turn,' he said, 'I beg you to listen to me. You wish to return whence you came, and I am not surprised at it, for I know that every effort has been made there to wrest you from me. It is a house of mourning and vengeance.... But you are not alone, remember; there is the child you bear, and you cannot take it from me in that way to hand it over to others.'

Geneviève was standing before her husband, who, on his side, leant against the door. She seemed to increase in stature, to become yet more resolute and stubborn as she cast in his face these words: 'I am going away expressly in order to take that child from you, and place it beyond the reach of your abominable influence. I will not have you make a pagan of that child and ruin it in mind and heart as you have ruined this unhappy girl here. It is my child, I suppose, and you surely don't mean to beat me under pretence of keeping it? Come, get away from that door, and let me go!'

He did not answer, he was making a superhuman effort to abstain from force, such as anger suggested. For a moment they looked at one another in the last faint gleam of the expiring light.

'Get away from that door!' she repeated harshly. Understand that I have quite made up my mind. You do not desire a scandal, do you? You would have nothing to gain by it; you would be dismissed and prevented from continuing what you call your great work—the teaching of those children, whom you have preferred to me, and whom you will turn into brigands with your fine lessons.... Yes, be prudent, take care of yourself for the sake of your school, a school of the damned, and let me return to my God, who, some day, will chastise you!'

'Ah! my poor wife,' he murmured in a faint voice, for her words had wounded him to the heart. 'Fortunately it is not you yourself who speak; it is those wretched people who are making use of you as a deadly weapon against me. I recognise their words, the hope of a drama, the desire to see me dismissed, my school closed, my work destroyed. It is still because I am a witness, a friend of Simon, whose innocence I shall soon help to establish, that they wish to strike me down, is it not? And you are right, I do not desire a scandal which would please so many people.'

'Then let me go,' she repeated stubbornly.

'Yes, by and by. Before then I wish you to know that I still love you, love you even more than ever, because you are a poor sick child, attacked by one of those contagious fevers, which it takes so much time to cure. But I do not despair, for at bottom you are a good and healthy creature, sensible and loving when you choose, and some day you will awaken from your nightmare.... Besides, we have lived together for nearly fourteen years, I made you wife and mother, and even though I neglected to re-mould you entirely, the many things which have come to you from me will continue to assert themselves.... You will come back to me, Geneviève.'

She laughed with an air of bravado. 'I do not think so,' she said.

'You will come back to me,' he repeated, in a voice instinct with conviction. 'When you know and understand the truth, the love you have borne me will do the rest; and you have a tender heart, you are not capable of long injustice.... I have never done you violence, I have constantly respected your wishes, and now, as you wish it, go to your folly, follow it till it is exhausted, as there is no other means of curing you of it.'

He drew aside from the door to make way for her, and she for a moment seemed to hesitate amid the quivering gloom which was enshrouding that dear and grief-stricken home. It had become so dark that Marc could no longer see her face, which had contracted while she listened to him. But all at once she made up her mind, exclaiming in a choking voice: 'Good-bye!'

Then Louise, lost amid the darkness, sprang forward in her turn, wishing to prevent her mother's departure: 'Oh! mamma, mamma, you cannot go away like this! We, who love you so well—we, who only want you to be happy——'

But the door had closed, and the only response was a last, distant cry, half stifled by a sound of rapid footsteps: 'Good-bye! good-bye!'

Then, sobbing and staggering, Louise fell into her father's arms; and, sinking together upon one of the forms of the classroom, they long remained there, weeping together. Night had completely fallen now, nothing but the faint sound of their sobs was to be heard in the large dark room. The deep silence of abandonment and mourning filled the empty house. The wife, the mother, had gone, stolen from the husband and the child, in order that th might be tortured, cast into despair. Before Marc's tearful eyes there rose whole machination, the hypocritical, underhand efforts of years, whic wrenched from him the wife whom he adored, in order to weaken h goad him into some sudden rebellion which would sweep both his work and himself away. His heart bled, but he had found the strength to accept his torture, and none would ever know his distress, for none could see him sobbing with his daughter in the darkness of his deserted home, like a poor man who had nought left him save that child, and who was seized with terror at the thought that she likewise might be wrested from him, some day.

A little later that same evening, as Marc had to conduct a course of evening lessons for adults, the four gas jets of the classroom were lighted, and students flocked in. Several of his former pupils, artisans and young men of modest commercial pursuits, assiduously followed these courses of history, geography, physical and natural science. And for an hour and a half Marc, installed at his desk, spoke on very clearly, contending with error and conveying a little truth to the minds of the humble. But all the time frightful grief was consuming him, his home was pillaged, destroyed, his love bewailed the lost wife whom he would find no longer overhead, in the room once warm with tender love, and now so cold.

Nevertheless, like the obscure hero he was, he bravely pursued his work.